The Summer Wedding

MARRIED IN MALIBU

BOOK 2

LUCY KEVIN

THE SUMMER WEDDING

Married in Malibu, Book #2

© 2017 Lucy Kevin

Sign up for Lucy's Newsletter

http://eepurl.com/hUdKM

www.LucyKevin.com

Jenn Fairhurst wants the Married in Malibu wedding cakes to be legendary. Her job baking sweet treats at the boutique Southern California wedding venue means everything to her. Even if she's not sure that she'll ever be able to love—or trust—a man again after going through a terrible divorce.

Daniel Brooker is an award-winning photojournalist who gave up his globetrotting career to become a wedding photographer after his wife passed away, leaving him as the sole parent to his son and daughter. After such a tragic loss, he never thought he'd be able to love again. Until he met Jenn.

Soon, Daniel is falling head over heels for Jenn and wants to show her what true love really is. But just when it looks like she might finally be ready to give love another try, her past comes back to haunt her. Will she be able to risk her heart again?

NOTE FROM LUCY

I absolutely love stories of second chances. Jenn and Daniel both have so much love to give—they've simply been waiting for the right person to give it to. This is something neither of them truly believed would happen...

But then, they met each other.

I hope you fall head over heels for their romantic and emotional story. I'm having so much fun writing this spinoff series from my *Four Weddings and a Fiasco* series, and I hope you love everyone at Married in Malibu as much as I do!

Please sign up for my New Release Newsletter at **www.LucyKevin.com/Newsletter** so that I can let you know when the next story in this fun and romantic new series is released.

Happy reading,
Lucy Kevin

Chapter One

The sun was starting to dip behind the ocean as Jenn Fairhurst put the last of the cakes into the oven to bake, then grabbed a piping bag to apply tiny rosettes of frosting to a lemon and raspberry cake. She'd been inside Married in Malibu's kitchen since dawn, and her T-shirt was dusted with flour, her jeans smudged with streaks of chocolate.

"Everything is looking—and smelling—really good in here," Daniel Brooker, Married in Malibu's photographer, said from the doorway. "Greta Sanserre is going to be blown away tomorrow when she comes to check us out for her wedding."

"I sure hope so," Jenn said with a smile. With a Golden Globe award and several recent blockbuster movies, Greta Sanserre was a very big deal. It would be a huge coup to book her wedding.

Jenn had always loved baking, but it had only been a hobby until she'd taken the job at the boutique wedding venue a month ago. She owed Rose and RJ, the owners, and her boss, Liz, everything for taking a chance on her. The very last thing she wanted to do was disappoint anyone here—she'd work until the sun came up again to prepare for tomorrow's meeting if that's what it took to create wedding cake magic.

"Is it all right if I take some shots of your cakes for the website and brochures?" Daniel asked.

"They're only test cakes." If she had been baking professionally for more than just the past few years, maybe she wouldn't be so nervous about the quality of her cakes. "And I'm not done decorating them yet."

"Actually," he said in his deep, steady voice that always made her feel warm and comforted, "it would be even better if I could get some shots of you in action putting on the finishing touches. Will that work?"

Though her heart beat faster at the mere thought of Daniel watching her through his lens, she said, "Okay. Just as long as you don't leave any fingerprints in the frosting. Otherwise," she teased, "there will be no more cupcakes for you."

Daniel often stopped by the kitchen throughout the workday, and she'd quickly learned that he had a particular fondness for her chocolate cupcakes. The time he spent hanging out in her kitchen made her feel like she was a part of the group, rather than shut away in her own little domain.

He moved into the kitchen with his cameras, flashgun, light meter, and tripod, promising, "You'll hardly know I'm here."

Jenn wasn't sure that was possible, given that whenever Daniel was nearby, she found it hard not to notice his presence. He was far too alive and animated to simply fade into the background, his eyes bright and intelligent as he looked at the world in ways other people couldn't.

He was at least six feet tall with rangy muscles beneath his clothes, and though he shot weddings for a living now, he still dressed like a photojournalist in shirts and pants that had plenty of pockets for spare camera equipment. He also had two really cute kids. Jenn had met them only briefly after Liz and Jason's wedding on the beach, but from what she could see, Kayla and Adam seemed like happy, well-brought-up children. It didn't hurt that, just like their father, they both loved her cupcakes.

Tonight, though Jenn was intent on making her cakes as perfect as she possibly could, it was nice to have a friend share her space. And as she moved from the refrigerator to the workbenches to the ovens, while he grabbed shots from every angle, it almost felt as though they were doing a special dance together.

Normally, she would have been working alone by this hour. Just her and the last batch of frosting. Actually, if she was already at that stage…

She looked around the kitchen, surprised to see how close she was to being done.

"Looks like you're not far off," Daniel said, echoing her thoughts. He held out his camera. "Take a look."

Jenn knew how much it meant that he was allowing her to look at his work in its raw, pre-edited form. She would have been worried about letting anyone taste her cakes before they were ready. After brushing the flour off of her hands so that she wouldn't damage his expensive digital camera, she took it from him to look at the photos.

"Wow." Her cakes seemed to shine and shimmer on the screen. She'd never thought anything she made could look that good. It had struck her more than once during the past month that Daniel took pictures as naturally as breathing, effortlessly documenting beautiful moments so that people could pin their happy memories in place forever. "You've made my cakes look like they're something out of a fairy tale," she said as she gave the camera back.

"You're the one who's done that, actually."

She was staring into his deep-blue eyes—and he was staring right back—when the oven timer went off. Working to act like her flushed cheeks were simply a result of working in a hot kitchen, she hurried to take the cake out and place it on a cooling rack on the counter. This last cake was about simplicity and elegance, a short culinary sprint to the finish line. She washed her bowls and pans while it cooled, then applied a layer of marzipan and a few smooth sweeps of frosting.

"I'm done," she said at last.

Suddenly exhausted, she sat down at the counter. Daniel sat beside her, offering her a bag of trail mix, which she munched gratefully. She hadn't realized how hungry she was until now. When she looked at her cakes laid out across the stainless-steel counters, relief swept over her.

"I can't believe they turned out so well."

"Why not? Your cakes are always beautiful." Daniel got up to take another few shots. "Although I have to admit that this time you've gone above and beyond. All this, and it's not even for the actual wedding, just the first meeting before she's even booked with us. You must be a big Greta Sanserre fan."

"Who isn't?"

It was so easy to feel comfortable around Daniel. Yet at the same time, *comfortable* wasn't really the right word for it. She could have sworn there had been sparks flying between them when she'd been staring into his eyes and he'd been looking back at her like he wanted to kiss—

No. She couldn't think like that. She and Daniel were simply co-workers and friends. Nothing more than that.

They couldn't be.

"What is it that's made you such a fan?" Daniel

asked.

It took her a moment to realize that he was talking about Greta Sanserre, not about her feelings for him. Another time, she might have said something about how much she enjoyed Greta's movies or the causes the actress was involved in. Tonight, however, Jenn didn't want to hold back the truth. Maybe it was because she was tired from a long day. Or maybe it was simply because he was quickly becoming a good friend.

"You heard about her first marriage, didn't you? How her husband cheated on her?"

"I'm pretty sure I read something about it in the papers."

"Well, after what happened with my ex-husband…"

Oliver had told Jenn he'd cheated only once, but for all she knew, it could have happened a dozen times with a dozen different women. Not that it mattered either way. All that mattered was that she'd come home to find her husband in bed with another woman, at which point she'd walked out of the house and begun divorce proceedings immediately. She knew how much an affair hurt—and how much effort it took to get over it.

Which was why she still hadn't managed it.

"I'm sorry he hurt you, Jenn."

She swallowed hard as Daniel's gentle words landed right in the center of her chest. "I just think it's really great that Greta has managed to find love again with someone else."

For a few long moments, Daniel simply held her gaze, his own unreadable. Finally, he said, "I agree. A second chance at love is definitely something worth making an effort for."

Chapter Two

Second chances.

After Daniel lost his wife, Victoria, to a car accident, he'd been convinced there would never be anyone else. There were women who were interested in him, but he never felt the same way. Never felt any real, lasting emotions for them. What's more, he couldn't bring just anyone into his kids' lives. Daniel not only wasn't sure how a woman would feel about stepping into a ready-made family, but he also wasn't sure how his kids would react to having someone new around.

But then he met Jenn...and everything changed. Changed so much that he started to wonder if he really could have a second chance at love.

The first moment he set eyes on her, a spark lit inside him. And as soon as they talked? He started falling head over heels for the sweet, intelligent, talented baker. The time they'd spent together since then continued to strengthen that initial flare of awareness and connection. Tonight, he'd been hard-pressed to concentrate on taking pictures when all he really wanted to do was kiss her. Unfortunately, she had been hurt so badly by her cheating ex that Daniel knew it might be impossible for her to trust someone again.

Every day for the past few weeks, the urge to tell her about his feelings grew stronger and stronger. But if she wasn't ready to hear it, wouldn't it make it difficult for them to work together day in and day out at Married in Malibu? Worse, could it ruin the friendship they'd built over the past month?

The buzzing of his cell phone in his pocket broke into his conflicted thoughts.

Dad, don't forget about the cupcakes for the fundraiser. They have to be homemade.

Love you, K

"What's wrong?" Jenn asked, obviously having caught Daniel's look of sudden dismay. "Are your kids okay?" She looked up at the clock on the wall in alarm. "I didn't mean to keep you at work so late."

"Don't worry, Mrs. Henderson from down the street looks after them when I'm not there. She's in her sixties, but she loves spending time with the kids. She's really helped a lot, and Kayla and Adam have grown close to her." He picked up his phone again, wondering how to break the news to his daughter that he'd completely dropped the cupcake ball. "Kayla was reminding me that we need to make homemade cupcakes tomorrow afternoon for a school fundraiser."

"When we were at Liz and Jason's wedding, Kayla asked me if I could come over sometime to show her how to do fancy frosting decorations on cupcakes." Jenn smiled. "I told her that I'd love to."

In Daniel's experience, people usually weren't interested in other people's kids. One of his former editors had gone even further, saying that he'd be a better photojournalist without kids holding him back, as though he expected Daniel to just abandon them. He'd quit the paper the next day.

"Does she have everything she needs for the cupcakes?" Jenn asked.

"In the whirl of weddings, school runs, and soccer practices, I completely forgot about the school fundraiser. So no, we don't have anything ready yet." And there was nothing Daniel hated more than letting his kids down.

"How many do you need to make?"

"A hundred," he said, suddenly feeling every pound of the weight of single-parenting on his shoulders. "I'll swing by the twenty-four-hour grocery store on the way home and pick up a bunch of boxes of cake mix."

"You don't need to use a mix. I'll help Kayla make the cupcakes tomorrow afternoon." Jenn smiled. "It will be fun."

"But you've spent all of today in the kitchen, and you're meeting with Greta tomorrow morning."

"I was planning to take tomorrow afternoon off after the meeting, but making cupcakes sounds way more fun. We'll need flour, and baking soda, and—"

"Jenn, you really don't have to do this."

"—at least three different flavorings for that many cupcakes."

She was as animated now making plans to bake cupcakes with Daniel's daughter as she had been preparing sample wedding cakes for a world-famous actress. Still, he knew he should try again to let her off the hook, even if that was the very last thing he wanted.

"You should be relaxing on your afternoon off, not baking a hundred cupcakes with my daughter."

"For me, a day spent baking *is* relaxing. And I want to help."

Daniel gave in with a grateful smile. "Thank you. I know Kayla will be happy to have you there."

And so will I.

"Tell me more about your kids." She grabbed a sponge to wipe down the counters. "They seem great."

"They are," Daniel said with a smile as he quickly sent his daughter a text with the good news that Jenn was on board to help with cupcakes, then began to pack up his camera equipment. "Kayla takes after her mom, always leading Adam around like a pint-sized adult, even though she's only nine. Sometimes I find her giving me these serious looks that I would expect from a kid twice her age. Adam's more like me, running around looking for adventure, but mostly just getting into trouble."

Jenn cocked her head. "I have a hard time imagining you getting into trouble."

"Ever since the kids came, I've tried to be a stable presence. But back when I was a photojournalist, things could get pretty nuts. I used to think that it wasn't a good story unless someone was chasing me away for trying to tell it."

"And now?"

"Now I feel like the best stories are the happy ones about people coming together and staying together."

"I agree. But do you ever miss your old job and the excitement of it all?"

"When I first left, I thought I might. But it turns out putting on weddings can be pretty exciting. And it's been great getting to watch my kids grow up in a nice neighborhood not far from their school, with friends and family close by. Plus," he added with a grin, "I don't get chased nearly as much anymore."

"Except by soccer moms," Jenn said in a low voice. When he looked at her in surprise, she blushed. "Did I just say that out loud?"

He grinned. Maybe she wasn't as immune to him as

it seemed.

Jenn waved her sponge-holding hand as if to wipe away what she'd just said, then refilled the spot with, "Kayla and Adam must keep you busy."

"They do, but it's the best kind of busy. Working at Married in Malibu instead of as a traveling photojournalist means I'm there to tuck them in for bedtime as often as I can. My family will always come first."

"Of course they do," she said in a soft voice. "Oliver and I were talking about having a family before—" Her face flushed with a combination of embarrassment and anger. "Before it all went wrong."

Just thinking about what her ex had done was enough to make Daniel's fists clench. He wanted to drag the guy in front of Jenn and force him to apologize to her. At the same time, Daniel wanted to make sure her ex never bothered her again.

"Sorry," she said with a shake of her head. "I don't mean to keep bringing it up. I guess working on Greta's sample cakes today got me thinking about how similar our situations were." Clearly wanting to change the subject, she added, "I really hope she likes the samples."

"As soon as she sees your cakes, she's going to want to book her wedding with us. And once she tastes one? She's going to *beg* us to work with her."

"You're so sweet." Picking up their things, they headed out of the kitchen for the parking lot. "But we both know Married in Malibu has so much more to offer than just my cakes. There's the beach, the security Travis offers, Nate's technical ingenuity, Kate's flowers, Margaret's designs, Liz's organizational skills—and, best of all, your incredible photos."

"I'm simply capturing the moment," he said, although the truth was that her admiration made him feel as if he'd just won a Pulitzer. "It's everyone at the wedding who helps to create the magic."

That had always been his philosophy as a photographer—he was there to capture the present moment, rather than to impose himself on the situation or create something that wasn't already there. To Daniel, the truth was extremely important. Which was just one more reason why Jenn's ex's betrayal was so bad. Daniel couldn't imagine lying like that to someone he loved. Especially when she was such a sweet and trusting person.

They were standing beside their cars by the time she said, "You always make it sound so easy, but we all know how much talent it takes not only to spot just the right moment that people will want to hold on to."

Jenn obviously noticed how hard he worked to frame those moments so that other people could see how beautiful, how full of wonder their lives truly were. But did she have any idea that from the moment he first met her, he'd seen all the joy hidden inside her shining through, rather than seeing only the quiet, reserved baker she was on the surface?

"I'm glad you were able to come in to take pictures tonight," Jenn said as they stood together beneath the Malibu moon. "It's made what would have been a long night a lot more fun."

"I'm glad too," Daniel replied, unthinkingly holding her smile until she blushed and looked away. Her keys jangled in her hand as she got into her car and waved good-bye, then drove away.

He hadn't meant to stare—he simply couldn't help it. Just the way he couldn't help falling more deeply for her with every passing second...

Chapter Three

Greta Sanserre was the image of Hollywood perfection as she walked into the Married in Malibu kitchen the following morning. Tall and slender, with coffee-colored skin and a dazzling smile, she looked as if she'd come straight from a fashion shoot.

"Jenn," Liz said, "I'd like to introduce Greta Sanserre. Greta, this is Jennifer Fairhurst, who designs and bakes our wedding cakes."

"It's a pleasure to meet you," the movie star said, holding out her hand. "Please call me Greta. Liz has been telling me that you can produce any cake combination I have in mind, and I can't wait to see—and taste—your samples. Although, I must warn you that I can be a little particular about things."

"It's lovely to meet you," Jenn said as she shook the woman's hand. As a matter of fact, she had heard that Greta Sanserre was a perfectionist. Evidently, the star had not only insisted on reshooting several crucial scenes on her last film, looking for the perfect take, but she'd also demanded that the sets on a period drama be overhauled because the historical details hadn't met her standards.

As Jenn uncovered her cakes, she silently prayed that Greta would like what she'd created. The other woman looked them over carefully for several seconds.

Finally, she said, "They're beautiful. Absolutely stunning."

Flushing slightly from the praise, Jenn cut a slice from the first cake and handed it to Greta on a small plate. The star bit into it, then closed her eyes and made a happy sound. Feeling hopeful, Jenn passed her a piece from another cake, and then another.

"Well," Greta said once she'd finished with her last taste, "I see why you brought me to the kitchen first, Liz."

Jenn couldn't keep from beaming. "I'm so glad you're pleased."

"Your wedding cakes are so delicious, Jenn, they're going to haunt my dreams." Greta turned back to Liz. "I feel confident with all the other details you've already explained to me, so if you have the contract with you, I'll sign it now."

While Greta flipped to the last page of the contract, Liz took a bottle of champagne out of the refrigerator. The pop of the cork came just as the star signed her name. When Jenn started this job, she had never expected to find herself sharing champagne with Hollywood royalty.

"I know Christopher is going to love Married in Malibu as much as I do," Greta said as she happily sipped from her glass.

Maybe it was drinking champagne on an empty stomach that made Jenn's next words tumble out. "I'm so happy for you and your fiancé. We're all going to do our best to make everything absolutely wonderful for both of you."

Greta put a hand on Jenn's arm and gave her a warm smile. "Thank you. That means a lot. It will be great to have my wedding at a place where I know people really care."

Liz and Greta left soon afterward to meet with the rest of the staff, and when Liz returned, alone, thirty minutes later, she was ecstatic.

"You did it, Jenn." Unexpectedly, her boss swept her up in a hug. "You're amazing. You know that, right?"

Amazing? *Her?*

When she was married, her baking had been just one of the many sources of arguments between Jenn and her husband. *Why are you wasting your time with that?* he'd always said. *You certainly don't need the extra calories, and I can't eat that garbage.*

As a personal trainer, he'd flatly refused to eat the things she baked, claiming that they would throw his blood-sugar levels out of balance. She'd ended up giving away the treats she made, first to family and then to friends. Eventually, people had started asking her if they could pay her to bake for their events and celebrations. But even when she began to make money with her hobby, Oliver hadn't been impressed. He was evangelical in his hatred of sugar, which meant Jenn's burgeoning business was nothing but shameful for him. Sometimes she felt like she was still shaking off that shame, even after one of the biggest movie stars in the world had just fallen into rapture over her cakes.

Thankfully, Liz didn't seem to be waiting for Jenn's response as she said, "Jason's coming to pick me up for lunch in a few minutes, but I wanted to be sure to tell you how much I appreciate having you here at Married in Malibu."

Flushed with pleasure at Liz's compliments, Jenn walked with her to the entrance. Jason Lomax, a bestselling thriller writer, was leaning against his truck in the parking lot, waiting for Liz. When he saw his wife, his entire face lit up. Moments later, he was sweeping her into his arms.

It was wonderful watching them together, how in love they were. Though they'd broken off their engagement a decade before, in the end they loved each other far too much for anything to stand in the way. Married in Malibu had brought them back together, and now that they were husband and wife, the happiness radiating from them was easy to see.

It was exactly the kind of happiness Jenn had once hoped to have herself. But after she'd left Oliver, she'd been so sure that she could never fall for anyone again.

Then again, she'd never counted on meeting Daniel.

Lost in her thoughts, she was heading back toward her kitchen to put everything away when she nearly ran headfirst into Margaret, who was carrying a huge stack of fabric swatches.

As usual, Married in Malibu's event planner looked far more chic than Jenn ever could. With her blond hair done up in a complicated braid and wearing a designer suit, Margaret was almost a match for the movie star who had just left. The big difference between Margaret and Greta Sanserre, however, was that the movie star never looked as tentative about things as Margaret often did.

"I heard you wowed Ms. Sanserre, Jenn. Great job."

"Thank you, I'm really pleased with how things went. But didn't she tell you to call her Greta when she met you?"

"She did, but it seems a bit informal."

"I'm sure she just wants us to feel comfortable around her." When Jenn saw that Margaret wasn't quite convinced, she added, "Don't your friends and family ever call you by a nickname?"

"Not my family, but my friends sometimes call me Meg. You can call me that if you'd like," she said softly. "And I'd love to hear more about your meeting with Greta. She couldn't stop talking about your cakes."

"She really did seem to love them," Jenn said, pride welling up inside of her again. "She tasted all of the samples, and the next thing I knew, Liz was popping champagne while Greta signed the contract."

"I'm not surprised at all." Meg's pretty face transformed into stunning beauty as she smiled. "You're the best baker I've ever known. And judging by the way everyone at Married in Malibu hangs around your kitchen begging for treats, they all clearly agree with me. Especially Daniel. Liz was joking the other day that he's made your kitchen his second office."

"What do you think of Daniel?" Jenn asked the question before she could stop herself. Maybe the champagne hadn't quite worn off yet. Or maybe it was because she'd been thinking about him constantly since last night— since the first time she'd met him, if she was being perfectly honest with herself.

"He seems very nice," Meg said. By her reserved standards, that counted as gushing praise. "And I've also noticed that he likes to spend time around you, even when you're not feeding him cupcakes." A beat later, her co-worker seemed to regret what she'd just said as she added, "Sorry, I know it isn't any of my business."

"I'm glad you feel like you can talk openly to me," Jenn reassured her, "because then I can be as open with you."

"Of course you can," Meg said, though she sounded surprised that Jenn would want to speak with her about matters of the heart. Surprised, but also pleased.

"Good," Jenn said with no small measure of relief, "because I feel like I've been bottling up my feelings forever."

"Feelings for Daniel?"

Jenn nodded. "I like being around him too—I *really* like it—but at the same time, I wouldn't want things to end up awkward here at work if things got messy. And I definitely wouldn't want to confuse his kids by being there one day and gone the next."

"Well..." Meg said slowly, drawing the word out as if trying to process everything Jenn had just dumped on her in the hallway. "I've started to realize that sometimes good things happen when you don't expect them to. I never dreamed I would be paid to put on dream weddings, and when Liz came to me with the opportunity, I nearly said no because I knew my family wouldn't approve. But then I realized that sometimes we have to take chances, even if we're not totally certain how they'll turn out. And working at Married in Malibu has worked out wonderfully so far."

"It has been good," Jenn said. "Amazing, actually.

Which is why I couldn't stand it if I ruined things at work by mixing business with—"

"No," Meg said, cutting Jenn off in an uncharacteristically firm tone. "That's not what I was trying to say. Honestly, I think you should keep an open mind about Daniel. He's a great guy, and the two of you would make a lovely couple."

"He hasn't asked me on a date," Jenn wanted to clarify, "but I am headed over to his house this afternoon to help his daughter bake cupcakes for school."

"His daughter's very lucky. I would have loved having someone help me with things like that when I was her age instead of having to figure everything out myself." As if she suddenly realized she'd given away too much about her past, Meg said, "I should be running back to my office now. Greta wanted to see a few changes to my sample boards for her wedding."

She was already setting off when Jenn called out, "Meg? Thank you. I really needed to talk things through with a friend today."

Meg's smile lit up her face again. "Anytime you need a friend, you know where to find me."

When Jenn had taken the job at Married in Malibu, she'd hoped to further her baking career. But she'd found far more than that. She'd found new friends who made her laugh. Friends who supported her dreams.

Friends who listened when she needed to talk.

And one very special friend who made her heart beat faster every time she thought about him.

Chapter Four

Daniel's house was in a great, family-friendly neighborhood, with a child's bright blue bicycle leaning against the side of the garage. Jenn parked her small hatchback behind the family minivan, but before she could retrieve her ingredients from the trunk, Daniel emerged from the house to help her take everything inside.

"Load me up with bags."

"Thank you." She smiled at him, and when he smiled back, it felt different than usual. She was still trying to figure out if that was okay, if she could let herself look at Daniel as more than a friend without hurting anyone—including herself.

Just then, Kayla bounded over to take the cupcake trays. "I'm so glad you're here!"

At nine, she was a couple of inches taller than her seven-year-old brother. She had blond hair that bounced around her shoulders with a life of its own, deep-blue eyes that reminded Jenn of Daniel's, and a heart-shaped face she must have inherited from her mother. She already had on a floral-printed apron, and it was clear that she couldn't wait for Jenn to come inside.

"Me too," Adam said in a slightly shy voice. He had the same blond hair and blue eyes that Kayla did, although his features more closely took after Daniel's. No doubt about it, all the girls at school were going to have crushes on him when he was older.

"They've been excited since they got home from school. Adam has been jumping around, while Kayla's been getting him to measure things out on the kitchen scales."

"What kinds of things?" Jenn asked.

"Pretty much anything they could find. Including most of the LEGO blocks in the house." He smiled at her again, and her heart went topsy-turvy inside her chest. "Congratulations, again, on blowing Greta away with your samples. I knew you would, but I had to leave to pick the kids up before I could find you for a celebratory hug."

Jenn flushed with warmth. Oliver would never have said anything so sweet, so complimentary. But then, Daniel was about as far from Oliver as it was possible to get, wasn't he?

"Can we bake now?" Adam asked. "Kayla said we'd have cupcakes."

"I said we'd *bake* cupcakes," his sister corrected him. "They're for school, remember?"

"Oh," Adam said, looking a little crestfallen.

Jenn couldn't leave him looking like that. "Don't worry, I bought enough ingredients to make extras."

With a whoop of joy, Adam led the way into the kitchen. Open and connected to the dining area, the kitchen had a marble-topped island, along with four stools and a window that looked out over a green backyard. To Jenn, it felt exactly like the warm family life she'd always dreamed of.

Smiling at the kids as she laid everything out on the counter, she asked, "Who wants to help me weigh the ingredients?"

Both of the kids did, of course, but thankfully they were happy to take turns. Where some big sisters might have bossed around a younger brother, Kayla seemed determined to support Adam by letting him learn on the job. His measurements were all good, until he started to explain something that had happened at school involving a frog and one of his teachers.

"And then Mrs. Simons was running around the room trying to catch it, and it was hopping everywhere!"

Though Jenn hadn't quite been able to follow the entire story, both kids' laughter was so infectious that soon she and Daniel were laughing too.

"We're going to make four different flavors of cupcakes," Jenn explained. "Vanilla, chocolate, strawberry, and carrot."

"Carrot?" Adam made a face.

"Some people will want healthy ones," Jenn said, scrunching up her face as she said *healthy* to make him laugh. "But don't worry, there will be plenty of chocolate cupcakes to make up for it."

They started mixing up the flour, eggs, baking soda, and milk. Jenn showed them how to add ingredients in bit by bit to avoid lumps as they stirred and how to tell if the mixture was the right consistency by watching the way it fell from their spoons.

As she put the cupcake trays into the oven to bake, Jenn silently noted how quickly, and easily, they'd all slipped into their roles this afternoon. Kayla was a fast study who picked up instructions well. When Jenn showed her how to construct a piping bag out of paper, Kayla had managed it perfectly after only two tries. Adam was a lot of help too, but seemed to be mostly interested in baking for the promise of cupcakes afterward. As for Daniel? After the second time he accidentally spilled most of a cup of flour on the floor, he had the sense to start taking pictures instead.

He was clearly devoted to his kids, complimenting Adam on how good he was at adding ingredients, while noting how quickly Kayla mastered constructing a piping bag. And the two of them seemed just as devoted to him.

"Do you really bake for a job?" Kayla asked Jenn.

"I really do. I make all of the wedding cakes at Married in Malibu."

Daniel's daughter looked quite impressed. "I didn't know that making cakes could be a job like how my dad takes pictures."

"I often have a hard time believing it myself," Jenn admitted. "Sometimes, it feels like my job's just a dream and that one day someone is going to force me to be an accountant instead."

"They can't really do that, can they?" Adam asked, taking a break from tasting the confectioner's cream they were preparing. He sounded more than a little worried about it.

"Of course they can't," Kayla assured him. "Jenn was just joking. Now, can we put the cream in the middle of the cupcakes? People are going to freak when they bite into these, they're going to be so good."

"You've got to be careful not to overfill them," Jenn explained, "or they'll ooze everywhere."

"Will they explode?" Adam asked in a hopeful voice.

"Only if you *really* overdo it," Jenn said with a laugh.

Soon, the first cupcakes were out of the oven. Once they cooled enough for decorating, Kayla proved a steady hand when it came to frosting. Adam was certainly enthusiastic...and Daniel wisely took care of ordering pizza.

"Are you married?" Adam asked suddenly.

Jenn nearly dropped the piping bag she was holding. With the kids looking up at her expectantly, she finally said, "Not anymore. I was married to a man named Oliver, but it didn't work out, and we ended up getting a divorce."

"Oh, just like Uncle Robbie did," Adam said before turning back to the cupcake he was decorating to look like a soccer ball.

Jenn was surprised to realize that where it could have been awkward to explain what had happened between her and Oliver, putting it in terms that a seven-year-old could understand—their marriage hadn't worked out, so they'd gotten a divorce—felt much more straightforward. Sensible, even.

With that out of the way, Jenn and the kids continued baking and decorating, while Daniel took more photos. Jenn was glad that the great memories the kids and their father made as a family would never be lost.

The doorbell rang, and a few minutes later the four of them were sitting around Daniel's living room table working their way through a family-sized pizza with extra pepperoni.

When they were done eating, Daniel said, "I hate to be a spoilsport, but it's getting close to your bedtimes."

"Aww...*Dad*," Kayla said. "Can't we at least finish making the cupcakes?"

"You've got other homework to do, don't you?"

Daniel asked.

"We've done it."

"Then why don't we go through it and make sure it's all okay?"

"But we're not done decorating yet and—"

"How about if I take care of the finishing touches on the remaining cupcakes?" Jenn suggested. "You and your brother have already done the hard work, so it won't be at all difficult to get everything ready to be taken to school."

Kayla considered that for a moment, then nodded. "Okay."

Jenn set to work finishing the cupcakes while Daniel helped Adam with questions on his math homework that he hadn't completely understood, and then he looked over Kayla's book report. When the kids went to brush their teeth and change into their jammies, Jenn couldn't help thinking again about how wonderful Daniel was with them. He was so patient, and it seemed like they would do just about anything for their dad. Even homework and flossing their teeth.

Daniel brought them back downstairs to say good night before tucking them in. Kayla rushed forward to hug Jenn, clinging tight and not letting go for a long time.

"Thank you for coming to help. Dad could never have made cupcakes like you."

"Like *us*," Jenn insisted as Adam came forward to hug her too. "We all did it together. And I had the best time."

"Me too," Adam said, squeezing her even tighter. "The best time *ever*."

* * *

Daniel's heart swelled as he watched his kids hugging Jenn. He longed to put his arms around her too, but he didn't want to make any missteps with her. She'd not only saved the day, but she had also been comfortable with his kids. She hadn't tried to do everything for them, but had trusted them to learn as they went.

The kids were reluctant to head to bed, obviously wanting to spend more time around Jenn, but after Daniel read them two short bedtime stories, they finally went to sleep. By the time he came back downstairs, he found Jenn setting out the last of the finished cupcakes on a baking tray.

"I'm all done," she said. "And those are for you and the kids."

Three extra cupcakes were sitting on the counter, two chocolate cupcakes for Adam and Daniel and a vanilla cupcake for Kayla.

"We could never have done this without you." He wanted to make sure she knew how much her time here today meant to all of them. "I'd still be floundering around, trying to work out how to mix the batter without it getting lumpy."

"Before tonight, I would have thought you were exaggerating, but now that I've seen you in action with the flour, I know you're being completely serious," Jenn teased. "Honestly, though, it's nice to know there's at least one thing that you can't do effortlessly."

She'd already packed up her things, so even though he wanted her to stay longer so that they could sit and talk some more, when she yawned, he made himself say, "Let me help you take your things back out to the car."

He reached for one of the bags just as she did. When their hands brushed, he not only wanted to revel in that sparking contact, he wanted to throw all caution to the wind and pull Jenn close enough to find out if her lips tasted as sweet as the ingredients for her cupcakes.

But though her eyes were bright and her cheeks flushed, he knew it was too soon when she shifted slightly back instead of forward. He wasn't going to back all the way off—how could he when his feelings for her were growing by leaps and bounds? At the same time, however, he needed to make sure he didn't overwhelm her.

After they'd stashed everything in her trunk, she said, "I really had a good time today. Thank you for letting me be a part of your family for a few hours."

There was so much he wanted to say, so much he

wanted her to know. But in the end, all he would allow himself to do was lean forward, give her a kiss on the cheek, and say, "You're a lifesaver, and the kids adore you." She was blushing again by the time he said, "I'll see you at work tomorrow. Drive safe."

She said, "Good night, Daniel," then got into her car and drove away, her hand resting lightly over the cheek he'd kissed.

Almost as if that kiss meant as much to her as it did to him.

Chapter Five

The next morning, Daniel arrived at Married in Malibu and headed straight to the main hall for the weekly meeting.

Kate was wiping smudges of potting soil from her hands, but had missed the stripe that had made it into her hair. She usually arrived early to work in the gardens—Daniel had never known anyone who had such a green thumb.

Travis was looking over several electronic security devices. The security consultant was easily the tallest, broadest figure in the room. As always, he was dressed in a well-pressed dark suit that still gave him plenty of room to move quickly if necessary.

Nate stood beside Travis, clearly impressed with the technology. He wasn't as broad as Travis, but he was nearly as tall, and wore work boots, jeans, and a plaid shirt. If Daniel didn't know better, he would think Nate worked construction rather than being Married in Malibu's IT expert.

Margaret, on the other hand, looked exactly the way he imagined a party planner would, in an elegant dress and expensive-looking shoes. She had a big leather notebook open and was making sketches while she waited for the meeting to get under way.

And then there was Jenn.

Daniel couldn't help but drink her in while she chatted with Kate. Kayla and Adam had repeatedly told Daniel how great they thought Jenn was. Of course, he already knew how much they'd loved having her over to make cupcakes with them. He'd always been careful about bringing someone new into his kids' lives, but it had felt so right to add Jenn into the mix yesterday. He wasn't at all surprised his kids had fallen for her so quickly. Just like he had.

He was tempted to walk over to her and tell her everything he was feeling. Just then, however, Liz arrived. She'd always been a cheerful person—and a great boss—but now that she and Jason were married, she simply glowed with happiness.

"Good morning," Liz said to the group. "As you all know, Greta Sanserre and her fiancé are our newest bride and groom!"

Everyone cheered. This was big news for Married in Malibu. The wedding for Jason's famous niece, Amber, had been a great start, but booking another one so quickly meant that they were keeping the momentum up. While their first wedding had come about partly because of Jason's connection, Greta had hired them based on their growing reputation and the great impression they'd made when she visited. Especially Jenn and her mouthwatering cakes.

"It truly is great news," Liz said, "and we all played a part in making sure that happened. But I want to give special thanks to Jenn. Your cakes were the clincher for this one. They convinced Greta that we would be able to exceed even her highest standards."

As far as Daniel was concerned, Jenn deserved all the praise that Liz could give her and more. Fortunately, one of the best things about Married in Malibu was that none of the others looked even the slightest bit jealous. Photojournalism was a cutthroat world—if one person got a front-page presence, it was at the expense of other photographers whose work would be used on less-visible pages. It was a side of his chosen field that Daniel disliked. The point of taking photographs, to him, was to tell a story about the important events taking place in the world—not whether he could get another photo credit to add to his résumé. Here, thankfully, everyone was on the same team.

"Well done," Margaret said to Jenn, with Travis, Nate, and Kate chiming in.

When Kate hugged Jenn, Daniel briefly wondered if he might be able to do the same. But he was afraid he would have a hard time stopping himself from doing more than just hugging her. Given that she was reddening at the praise from the others, he suspected she wouldn't react well if he kissed her in front of everyone.

"There's still a lot of hard work to do," Liz reminded them. "This wedding isn't in as short a timeframe as our first two—"

"I hope not," Nate put in. He was grinning as he added, "An afternoon to put on your wedding was pretty quick, even by our standards."

On a laugh, Liz continued. "But Greta will definitely notice if we don't get all the details exactly right. She has sent me her list of what she wants included in the wedding. A long list. With that said, Greta also wants us to 'use our creativity.'"

"Just to be clear," Margaret said, "we're all to be as creative as possible, but without getting any of the details that Ms. Sanserre—" She flushed slightly. "I mean, that Greta wants wrong?"

"Exactly," Liz replied. "But don't worry, most of what she has asked for are specific details, which leaves a lot of scope for each of your personal touches."

Liz was about to hand everyone a copy of the list when Travis said, "Are you sure you don't want to give each of us only the parts we need to see? I trust everybody in this room, but the more full copies there are of her requirements, the more chance there is that if something leaks, *everything* leaks."

"I understand your concern, Travis, but it's important for each of you to make choices that will fit in with the whole event, even the parts that aren't your responsibility. Remember, we'll always do our best work as a team rather than as a group of people doing things their own way."

Again, Daniel couldn't help thinking back to his days in photojournalism, where almost everyone was in it only for themselves. Married in Malibu was a breath of fresh air. In more ways than one, he thought, as he stole a glance at Jenn.

"I have one other piece of good news before we head off to start working on Greta's wedding," Liz said. "This morning, I received an email from *Brides* magazine."

A ripple of anticipation passed around the room. Even a one-line mention in the magazine would be a huge boost to Married in Malibu's reputation.

"Their next issue is going to focus on wedding cakes, and one of the bakers they had lined up flaked out at the last minute. Something about getting a better offer from reality TV."

Daniel could see where this was going, and from the way Jenn suddenly tensed up, it was obvious that she could as well.

"They've rearranged their photo shoot for a week from now, and they'd like to showcase your cakes,

Jenn."

Everyone exclaimed about what great news it was. Everyone but Jenn, who seemed more than a little shocked.

"A week?"

"I know it's tight," Liz said, "but with the other baker pulling out, they're already past their original deadline."

"If they're going to crash the pictures into the magazine at the last minute," Daniel said, "that presumably means that they know what open spaces they're looking to fill. Knowing the parameters going in will hopefully make it easier to plan for those final shots."

"Exactly," Liz said with a nod. "Jenn, do you think you can put some wedding cakes together in time for the shoot?"

Jenn's face was pale. "I..."

"Sure you can," Nate offered. "After all, you did such a great job with the sample cakes for Greta."

"I agree," Liz said. "Your cakes convinced a major movie star to book with us. If we can get pictures of them into a major magazine, just think how many other celebrities would feel the same way." Daniel could see that his boss didn't want to put undue pressure on her employee—but it was also clear that she believed Jenn was more than up to the challenge. "So, can you do it?"

Jenn didn't reply immediately. In fact, Daniel was

holding his breath by the time she finally nodded and said, "Yes. I'll do it."

"Great, I'll email *Brides* immediately to let them know and to get us the specifications for the photo spread." Liz obviously didn't want to give Jenn a chance to change her mind. "Daniel, while I know you're going to have some prep to do for Greta's wedding, since the photo shoot will take place first, I'd appreciate it if you could work closely with Jenn this week on creating the kind of cakes that will photograph best for the magazine."

Daniel didn't even try to hold back his grin. "I'd be happy to do that."

Happy wasn't nearly a good enough word to describe what he was feeling. He wanted Jenn's work to get all the recognition it deserved. And if it meant that they would need to spend the next week working closely together?

It was everything he could have hoped for.

Chapter Six

After the meeting broke up, Jenn knew she should head to the kitchen right away to begin planning her cakes for the magazine. Instead, she stood frozen in the middle of the hall, panicking about the super-short editorial deadline, about half the world staring at her cakes from the glossy magazine spread, and most of all about baking with Daniel.

"Why don't we head over to Tamara's café for a few minutes?" Meg suggested.

Jenn nearly threw her arms around her co-worker in relief. Especially given that she'd need the caffeine to make sure she was alert and creative when she started working on the new cakes.

Though she'd been exhausted by the time she'd returned home last night, she'd barely been able to sleep. How could she sleep when every time she closed her eyes she thought about how playful and loving Daniel was with his kids? And when she couldn't stop imagining what it would be like to kiss him?

Would his kisses be sweet and gentle? Heated and passionate? Or all of the above?

As the two women walked across the street to Malibu T & Coffee, Jenn tried to get out of her head long enough to appreciate the beautiful day. The sun was out, the sky was blue, and the air smelled like flowers in bloom. The café was booming with both tourists and locals, but despite the crowd, Tamara smiled at them as they came in. The team from Married in Malibu had rapidly become her best customers. Nate alone probably increased her profits by twenty percent.

Tamara was a tall, tanned—and beautiful—advertisement for Southern California beach life, dressed in bright fabrics with jangling jewelry. When Jenn ordered a latte, Tamara said, "Are you sure? From the way you keep yawning, I'd say you probably need something stronger." Her eyes gleamed with the obvious spark of wanting to mix up something special.

Normally, Jenn would be happy to try something new, but today she simply wanted to make it through the day. "A latte is fine."

"Spoilsport." But Tamara was grinning as she said it. A few minutes later, she left her assistant at the register and joined Jenn and Meg at their table. "Are you working on another big wedding that you're not allowed to tell me anything about?"

"There is one of those," Jenn admitted.

"There's also a big project for *Brides* magazine," Meg said excitedly. "They want to include Jenn's cakes in a special feature."

"Wow." Tamara hugged Jenn. "That's incredible."

"It's only because someone else pulled out," Jenn pointed out.

Tamara shook her head. "It sounds like someone is being far too modest. Isn't she, Margaret?"

"Absolutely." She looked shy as she said, "And please call me Meg. Margaret feels too formal for friends."

Tamara gave her a brilliant smile. "Meg it is, friend."

Jenn had dreamed of a job like this for so long. But now that she had a wedding to prepare for *and* a magazine shoot happening at the same time, she couldn't help but feel overwhelmed. And when she added in her budding feelings for Daniel?

Overwhelmed didn't even scratch the surface.

"I just can't believe this is happening. There are so many amazing bakers around the country. Why me?"

"They obviously think the work you did on Amber and Robert's wedding was amazing," Meg said. "I know it's going to be a lot of work, but aren't you at least a little bit excited about it?"

"Of course I am." Jenn flashed her friends a small smile. "I just don't want to let anyone down at Married in Malibu."

"You won't," Meg said as if it was the most obvious

conclusion in the world. "And don't forget, Daniel is going to be helping you in any way he can."

"Daniel's going to be 'helping,' is he?" Tamara grinned. "I can certainly think of worse people to be locked in a kitchen with."

Jenn could feel herself flushing as she said, "We're just going to be working together."

"That's what I said."

"No, you didn't," Jenn shot back. "You think I don't know quotation marks when I hear them?"

Tamara's grin only widened. "You have to admit, you do have some pretty cute guys working at Married in Malibu. Daniel has the whole family man thing going on, Travis is muscle from head to toe, and Nate...well, a girl can't be blamed for looking when there's so much to appreciate right in front of her."

Any other time, Jenn would have waded in to ask for more details about where Tamara was looking, especially when it came to Nate. Now, however, her brain felt so muddled that all she could manage was a rather prim, "I'm simply trying to concentrate on doing my best work."

"Anyone who takes a job at a wedding venue must be a romantic at heart," Tamara declared. "At least secretly."

Meg suddenly looked uncomfortable—as if she didn't want to get caught in a discussion of how much romance she did, or did not, have in her heart. "Do you have any ideas about what you might do for the shoot, Jenn?"

"Not yet. I want something that's going to show off what I can do and look good for Married in Malibu, but I don't know anything about photography. What if I make a great cake and it looks terrible on camera?"

"That's why Daniel is there."

"One reason he's there, at least," Tamara said with a waggle of her eyebrows. Before Jenn could insist again that it was just work, Tamara added, "You make your living baking and decorating cakes, and I make a good portion of mine watching people. And I've seen the way Daniel looks at you."

Jenn knew when she was beat. Because she'd been looking at him in exactly the same way.

"Maybe," she finally admitted.

Tamara practically jumped up from the table in excitement. "I knew it!" She was grinning from ear to ear. "Score one for my finely honed barista senses."

Jenn wished she could believe romance was all sunshine and rainbows. But she'd made that mistake before. Which was why she had to hedge her bets by saying, "The fact that he and I work together can't be a good thing, can it? Liz wouldn't like it if I ended up causing trouble at Married in Malibu before our next big wedding."

"First of all," Tamara replied, "they say that most romances start in the workplace." She looked briefly at her nineteen-year-old employee at the register. "Which, admittedly, doesn't give *me* a lot of hope, but in your case, that means the possibility of dating a hot photographer. And second, there will always be a next big wedding. So what are you going to do? Shove away your feelings forever? Plus," she continued, "Married in Malibu's last wedding was between Liz and your first client's uncle. And then there's Rose and RJ, the founders of the whole operation. They met at work, so I hardly think anyone at Married in Malibu would complain if you and Daniel decided to date."

"Maybe…" But even after the great time she'd had at Daniel's house making cupcakes with his kids, Jenn felt terribly conflicted about the situation. She just didn't want to make any more missteps when it came to love.

Not after getting it so wrong with Oliver.

Tamara pinned her with a very direct look. "Mixing work with pleasure isn't what you're really worried about, is it?" She didn't wait for Jenn to reply before pushing even further. "So spill. What's the *real* reason you're so worried about starting a relationship with Daniel?"

Jenn couldn't lie to her friends. Especially not when she knew that Tamara was going to keep asking until she knew everything. "I'm scared, okay? Things didn't work out with Oliver. What if this all goes wrong too? I don't think I could recover if I put my heart into another relationship and it all fell apart."

"I've never met your ex, but I'm still positive that Daniel is nothing like him," Meg said in a gentle voice. "Daniel is a great guy who would never want to hurt you."

"He is great," Jenn said. "He's sweet. And talented. And amazing with his kids. But I thought at first that Oliver was great too."

She'd been swept away by her ex, swept up in him. Even when things had started to go off the rails, she'd told herself that he was a good man and she simply needed to give him time to come around.

Until she'd found him in bed with another woman and realized just how wrong she'd been about everything.

"How can I ever really be sure about someone else when I missed all the signs before?"

"That's one of the benefits of working with Daniel on the *Brides* magazine cakes for the next few days," Tamara said. "You'll get to see so much more of him than you normally would—especially in the middle of a stressful deadline. If you can bring out the best in each other this week, then maybe that means the two of you truly are meant to be together. From what I've seen so far," she added as she put her hand over Jenn's, "I'd bet my last dime on it."

"I would too," Meg said, covering Jenn's other hand with hers.

Chapter Seven

At Travis and Nate's request, Daniel had spent the morning playing the part of a paparazzo trying to sneak into Married in Malibu. Intent on airtight security for their celebrity guests, they wanted to spot any possible place where someone might be able to get a good shot with a telephoto lens so that they could block the sight line. He'd enjoyed running around the grounds trying to elude Travis's best attempts at security, but at the same time, every minute helping them was one Daniel wasn't spending with Jenn.

It was one p.m. by the time he was able to head to the kitchen with his camera gear. Jenn was sitting at one of the worktops, a sketchbook open in front of her and the faintest wrinkle to her nose as she scribbled away.

When she eventually noticed him and started slightly, Daniel said, "Sorry, I've spent so much of the morning sneaking around pretending to be paparazzi for Travis and Nate that I'm having trouble making much noise right now."

Jenn laughed. "I'll bet your training as a photojournalist also makes you good at sneaking up on people, doesn't it?"

"The best is when I can get the kids to jump out of their chairs at home," he said with a grin. "Speaking of the kids, Kayla and Adam both think you are amazing." He wanted to tell her *he* thought she was amazing, but he knew the last thing he should be risking right now was making her uncomfortable before they began working closely for the next week.

"I think they're amazing too. And so are you." Her eyes widened as she scrambled to amend her statement. "What I mean is that you're a wonderful father."

She couldn't know how much that meant to Daniel. More than anything, he wanted to be a good father. Especially given that he was doing it all by himself. "They keep asking me when you can come back."

"I'd love to. It's just…" She bit her lip. "Finding the time right now for anything other than this shoot is going to be tricky, isn't it?"

He tried not to frown, not sure he bought the reason she'd just given him. "The schedule is pretty tight," he made himself agree.

He was trying to read her expression—was she on to his feelings for her and wanted him to back off?—when she said, "Your wife would be so proud of them, and you. She must have been a truly amazing, beautiful person, if the kids you had together are anything to go by."

"She was," Daniel replied.

Victoria had brightened up a room just by walking into it. She had been funny, kind, and beautiful. Every day, Daniel looked at his kids and saw reminders of their mother in their expressions, or the way they behaved. It was why he'd never dared to believe that there might be someone else out there for him.

Until he'd met Jenn.

Suddenly, all the warnings he'd been giving himself about taking things slow didn't seem to matter. He needed to tell her what he was feeling. Needed to know if she might one day feel the same.

"Jenn—"

"Daniel—"

"You first," he said, hopeful that she was thinking along the same lines.

"I was just going to say that we should probably get going on our game plan for the cakes, shouldn't we?"

Disappointment settled deep in his gut, even though he'd known better, hadn't he? She wasn't ready yet. Just because he felt closer to her every minute they were together didn't mean he could rush her into anything.

Forcing himself to turn his focus back to work, he gestured to her notebook. "It looks like you've been working through some ideas."

She turned her notebook so that he could see the paper filled with a few crossed-out sketches. "Normally, I'd be full of ideas. But I can't stop worrying about how the photo shoot will change things."

"Don't forget, your cakes looked great when I photographed them before Greta came in."

"You're right," she acknowledged with a smile. "Your photos were wonderful. But those were just simple sample cakes, not something on the scale that Brides magazine surely wants."

"I don't think you're going to have any problems knocking their socks off," Daniel said. "But if it will make you feel better to have some pointers, here's the most important thing to remember: The cakes have to be very visual since people reading the magazine won't be able to taste them. I've known some food stylists to use painted wooden and plastic models in place of the real food, because they're easier to photograph."

"I could never do anything like that," Jen said, looking horrified.

"I'm not suggesting you should." That was when an idea struck him. "What if we made a big deal out of the fact that your cakes are one hundred percent natural? I could document the process of you making them, and then we could show pictures of the cut slices so that people know you can produce great results without resorting to tricks of the camera. Even if the magazine decides not to use the photos, we can still put them up on the Married in Malibu website."

"I love that idea."

Just like that, they were off and running, discussing ideas, exploring potential pitfalls and working out solutions. When he wondered aloud if the heat from studio lights might affect the frosting, she created half a dozen different batches to try to find a recipe that wouldn't melt. And when she wanted to know about the effects of lighting on color, he applied different filters in his editing software to allow her to see potential changes. While they worked, they wove around each other in a dance of photos and baking that seemed to spark new ideas at every step. Too many ideas...

"Maybe if we both relax a little, the perfect idea will finally land." He looked out the window. "How about a short walk along the beach?"

The cove was a part of the Married in Malibu grounds, which meant that it was quiet and untouched by both tourists and locals. It was not only the perfect spot for a private beach wedding, it also made a great place for an afternoon break.

A few minutes later, they were walking along the sand. The sun was shining, the sky was cloudless, and the ocean rolled in and out in a steady, soothing rhythm.

"This beach is perfect," Jenn said.

It's even more perfect because you're here, he thought,

wanting to say the words aloud, but knowing it was too soon. Forcing himself to look away from her beautiful face, he bent to pick up an intricately patterned shell, then positioned it on the sand so that he could snap a picture of it. A few moments later, Jenn found a shell of her own to add to the arrangement. Pretty soon, they were crafting a complex and ever-expanding pattern. Daniel reached down for another shell…and Jenn's hand covered his as she reached for the same one.

Looking up, he realized she was only a few inches away. If either of them moved forward, their lips would touch. He held his breath, waiting to see if she would lean forward to close the gap. Instead, she straightened— and the moment disappeared as if made of smoke.

"I know what cakes I should make," she said suddenly. "One that's one hundred percent Malibu with a beach, the ocean, and seashells for decoration. One that's totally classic, such as a five-tiered wedding cake. And then, for a last one, I could put together a theme-park cake to further reinforce our Southern California location and the stars that become our clients."

Jenn's vision was so good that Daniel was momentarily diverted from his dashed hopes over the kiss that hadn't happened. They immediately headed back to her kitchen so that they could begin to work out all the details. They dug in with such enthusiasm, in fact, that he was surprised by the alarm on his phone that he'd set to make sure he made it home in time to get dinner on for the kids.

"I almost kept you late again, didn't I?"

"No," he assured her, "everything's fine. My parents have been watching the kids today, but they're going to the symphony this evening, so I need to head back."

"Thank you for a wonderful afternoon."

"It was pretty great, wasn't it?"

Suddenly, they were hugging. It was hard to say which of them started it. Perhaps they both simply had the idea at the same moment. Either way, Daniel loved feeling Jenn's warmth, her soft curves, pressed against him.

And he hoped she loved being in his arms just as much.

Chapter Eight

Jenn couldn't stop thinking about her cake designs. She made plans in the shower. She filled a half-dozen pages in her notebook while grabbing a bite to eat. Even her dreams had been invaded with visions of frosting and fillings, piping and chocolate.

Daniel had been in every one of her dreams too.

"Get a grip on yourself—you have cakes to make," she told herself as she walked into the Married in Malibu kitchen the following day. It was still hard to believe that this incredible space was her domain.

In order to meet the demands of both the *Brides* spread and Greta Sanserre's upcoming wedding, Jenn needed to give one hundred percent focus to her job. However conflicted she was by her feelings for Daniel, she still had baking to do.

Deciding to work on the traditional cake first, she reviewed the list she'd made the night before of the best options for each of the five tiers. Red velvet cake and chocolate were a must, of course, along with a plain sponge. A fruit cake might create a good contrast with texture. The same went for a polka dot cheesecake. She'd written down close to a dozen options, and she would soon have to narrow them down. For now, however, she would let herself experiment with different combinations to see what looked the best.

Daniel would be a huge part of this process, of course. His years of photographic experience were not only invaluable, but she also sensed that she was going to need to lean on him at least once during the week for moral support. Having seen him with his kids, she knew for sure that no one was a better cheerleader.

Eggs, flour, milk, water, food coloring, cocoa—Jenn was tallying up the amounts she was going to need when her phone pinged with a text.

Was it Daniel? Had he woken up thinking about her, the way she'd woken up thinking about him? Had he gotten his kids ready for school, dealt with the breakfast chaos, then decided to send her a quick *good morning* even before getting into the office?

But when Jenn checked her phone, the text wasn't from Daniel.

It was from her ex.

Her heart sank at the sight of Oliver's name. What could her ex-husband possibly want when she hadn't heard anything from him in months? One of his few redeeming qualities was that as soon as she'd asked him for a divorce, he'd disappeared almost completely, which had given her the space she'd needed to start to rebuild her life.

What could Oliver need at this time of the morning? Not only had he never been an early riser, but he'd always complained when she got up early to bake. She felt a little sick as she swiped her finger across the screen to read his message.

I know it's been a long time and things were difficult, but I'm on a totally new path that has turned my life around. Can I see you? It's important.

Jenn rolled her eyes. After all this time, Oliver thought he could just text to get her to meet him to discuss something "important"? And everything was about him, as usual. She texted back:

I'm completely tied up. Will be in touch when I have some time.

"Good morning, Jenn."

Her heart fluttered as she looked up from her phone to find Daniel standing in the doorway holding coffee and croissants. "I brought breakfast, just in case bakers are like shoemakers, who are always barefoot."

Normally, she would have laughed at his adorable— and correct—analogy. But even one short text from Oliver had been enough to bring the pain surging back.

Not just the pain of finding him in bed with another woman, but the pain of realizing he'd been lying to her for so long before that—and the way he'd constantly dismissed everything Jenn had wanted to do with her life. Even Daniel's presence couldn't make that hurt go away instantly.

"You're right that bakers do often go without breakfast," she confirmed with a shaky smile. "Thank you for thinking of me."

He put the coffee and croissants on a worktop so that he could reach out to put a hand on her shoulder. "Are you okay?"

A part of her wanted to spill everything. But she couldn't stand the thought of her ex intruding on her time with Daniel. "I'm a little tired. I got here a bit earlier than I intended."

"Eager to get to work?" Daniel guessed with a smile that made her heart go pitter-patter.

"Absolutely." She forcefully pushed thoughts of Oliver away. "We've got a lot to do today."

While they had decided on the core designs, and she had been thinking about recipes, there were still the basic cakes to bake, components to construct and fit together, props for displaying them to craft, and of course, figuring out how to make sure everything photographed beautifully.

"Don't worry," Daniel said as if he could read the

laundry list of rather daunting tasks in her head. "We'll get through it all. One thing at a time."

Knowing he was right, she took a deep breath, then said, "Okay, then, here is my list of ideas of cakes to use for the five different layers of the tiered cake. What jumps out at you?"

"I like the idea of a lot of color contrast, but the fruit cake might still work."

"Maybe if I incorporated a walnut swirl into it?"

Daniel nodded. "That would be good. That extra bit of visual impact would show people that your cakes aren't just about the decoration, even though they're going to be beautiful too."

Beautiful, but also a great deal of work. Each unique cake mix required different materials, ingredients, and timings. She was trying to work out how to manage the process when Kate poked her head into the kitchen. This was a rarity. Although Married in Malibu's gardener was fun to be around, she spent nearly all her time outside with her plants.

"I thought I'd come in to see if you needed any help." At Jenn's surprised look, Kate explained, "I know my way around a kitchen pretty well, since I do so much with the vegetables from my home garden."

"I'd love your help." Considering how many cakes Jenn needed to bake before Daniel could even begin to take test photos, that was the understatement of all time.

"But I don't want to pull you away from your work in the garden."

"I have a delivery of topsoil coming this afternoon, but before that I don't have all that much on my plate today."

"You know what?" Daniel's eyes had lit up with an idea. "It would be great to get some pictures with both of you working together. Not every workplace is full of supportive co-workers, so it might be nice to show on our website that ours is."

Wasn't it just like Daniel to put it so sweetly? "I agree wholeheartedly," Jenn said with a smile. "Our team here is amazing." She turned to Kate. "Can you start measuring ingredients for the sponge cake? I'll pull up the recipe for you on my tablet."

As Kate got to work, Jenn was pleased that she really did know her way around the kitchen. With Kate's help, the timeline might actually be manageable.

After snapping dozens of shots of the two of them in action, Daniel said, "We're going to need some backgrounds to show the cakes against. I'll be right back." A few minutes later, he returned with Nate, who looked happy as ever to step away from his computer and help out with a project. The two men mocked up simple backdrops from cardboard and paint, then called in Meg to lend her design expertise to the effort.

Over the course of the day, the kitchen got busier

and more crowded. Travis helped press dents out of the seashell molds Jenn wanted to use. Kate continued to help with the mixing, and even Liz dropped in, presumably to check that everything was going okay.

Eventually, however, Kate had to go take care of her topsoil delivery. Travis and Nate needed to finish testing the security cameras covering the remaining blind spots around the grounds. And Liz went with Meg to interview linen suppliers for the Sanserre wedding.

Jenn had thought she and Daniel would be spending the entire day alone, only to be surrounded by their friends and co-workers all day. And yet, every moment she'd still been aware of how great it felt having him near—and how sweet and helpful he was as he did everything he could to make the process seamless for her.

She went to get a cake out of the oven and yelped. "Ow!"

"Are you okay?" Daniel was by her side in an instant. When he saw the burn, he quickly grabbed a first aid kit from the corner of the kitchen, gently took her hand to soak it in cool water, then bandaged it carefully.

But Jenn barely noticed the sting of the burn on her skin. The only thing she could focus on was how electric his touch was.

"Is everything okay?" Liz asked as she suddenly appeared at the kitchen door.

"Just a minor baking injury," Jenn told her boss.

Liz rushed forward. "Are you sure you're okay?"

"I'm fine," Jenn assured her. In fact, this close to Daniel, with her skin still tingling from his touch, she was *more* than fine.

It was then that she saw the two women behind Liz. They looked like they'd come from an expensive spa.

"I thought that since you and Daniel are doing such a great job and working so hard," Liz said, "you should have a chance to relax before jumping into day three. Cindy and Adele are masseuses. Enjoy."

She left before Jenn could even thank her, and one of the masseuses stepped forward. "I'm Cindy. Liz booked head, neck, and shoulder massages for both of you. Would you like to sit down?"

Beyond surprised by this lovely gift at the end of what had been a very long day, Jenn sat on one of the special massage chairs the therapists had brought while Daniel took the other. She initially tensed when the masseuse began to press into her tight muscles, but soon relaxed under the woman's expert touch. Beside her, Daniel also seemed to be rapidly de-stressing.

"It's nice working on you both side by side," Cindy said, pushing at the knots in Jenn's shoulders. "Couples don't take enough time to just relax together."

"We're not a cou—" Jenn began, but the masseuse chose that moment to do something that made all her tension melt away.

Besides, it was impossible not to feel close to Daniel after they'd worked together so easily the past few days—both at Married in Malibu and at his house with his kids.

By the time the masseuses were done, she could barely summon the energy to move out of the chair so that the therapists could pack up and leave.

That was when she finally looked around the kitchen again and saw it all with new eyes. The basic cakes were done, they'd started work on the settings, and while there was still a huge amount of effort to put in, the *Brides* project didn't seem nearly as daunting as it had twelve hours ago.

"Did we really get all this done today?"

Daniel nodded. "We make a good team."

"Yes," Jenn agreed, unable to do anything but stare into his eyes. "Yes, we do."

And then, just as he had the previous day, he hugged her. She felt like she was completely wrapped up in him in the best possible way.

Their hug seemed to go on forever, neither of them willing to break it. When they finally did draw back, he said, "I think we should make an end-of-the-day hug a regular thing."

"Sounds good," Jenn said with a smile so wide, she knew she must look like a total goof. But how could she help it when she felt happier than she had in a very long time?

Because a regular end-of-the-day hug with Daniel didn't just sound good.

It sounded *amazing*.

Chapter Nine

Both Daniel and Jenn arrived at Married in Malibu early the next morning. When he pulled out coffee and pastries again, she said, "You're so sweet, but you don't have to keep going to Tamara's to pick up breakfast."

"I figured you'd prefer it to something I might bake myself."

Laughing, she said, "We can always give you another shot in the kitchen sometime, if you'd like." She broke off a piece of still-warm croissant and popped it into her mouth. "I really do appreciate how thoughtful you are. If every guy were like you, women wouldn't need to have so many girls' nights to drown our sorrows in bottles of wine." She scrunched up her nose in that adorable way she had when she wished she could take back her words. "What I meant to say is, why don't we go over our plan for the day?"

He wanted to say something that would make her feel better about her dog of an ex, but she seemed determined to put it behind her and get to work. Following her lead, he helped uncover each of the cakes she'd baked the day before.

"I'd like to get a base layer of icing down on each of the tiered layers," she told him. "I'd also like to sculpt the shape of the Malibu cake so that we have a recognizable seashore. When both of those things are done, I plan on baking a few components for the theme cake."

Many people would have already folded under the timeline, pressure, and expectations, but Jenn simply threw her heart into her work.

"I'll set up my angles and document everything you're working on, without getting in your way. Does that sound good?"

The smile she gave him turned everything inside of him warm. Joyful too. "It sounds great."

She began by whipping up batches of icing, working to find the perfect consistency and color. When that was done, she started on the detail-oriented process of sculpting her seashore cake into as perfect a replica of the cove as she could achieve. Daniel did his best to help by running down to the beach to snap photographs for her to work from. The people at *Brides* would never know if she had the topography right or not, but if it mattered to Jenn, then he was going to do whatever he could to make sure she nailed her vision.

"The slope is different from the way I imagined it," she said a short while later as she studied one of the photographs. She made a quick slice with a knife, shaving off a fraction of the sponge cake with great concentration.

Daniel couldn't stay in the kitchen all day, however, because Meg needed him to photograph several possibilities for the Sanserre wedding sets. For a couple of hours, he went back and forth between taking pictures of Jenn's progress in the kitchen and Meg's changing sets.

"How are you both doing?" Liz asked around lunchtime, bringing in sandwiches from Tamara's café.

"It's all going fine," Jenn assured her.

"We're great," Daniel echoed.

"Yes, I can see that." The way Liz smiled as she said it made Daniel wonder if she was referring to the magazine prep...or something else entirely. "The two of you should make sure to take a break now and then, especially considering that you were here even earlier than I was. I don't want you burning out."

"You already treated us to those incredible massages last night," Jenn said. "You really are the best boss in the world."

"I agree," Daniel said. "Back in my previous life, being sent into a war zone to take pictures was considered my reward for work well done. A massage beats that by a mile."

"Well, considering the two of you are a big part of why Married in Malibu is soon going to be known as the best wedding venue in the world, I'm more than happy to reward your excellent work. But I am serious about taking breaks."

"She's right, you know," Daniel said after Liz left. "You've been working nonstop since six this morning. You should take a break, at least for lunch. Kate's gardens are in full bloom. Why don't we eat outside?" It wasn't the same as asking her out on a date, but he hoped it was a step in the right direction, at the very least.

"I guess there isn't anything that will burn while we're away. And it would be nice to grab a little sun."

Married in Malibu's gardens were spectacular in their variety, a half-dozen microgardens rolled into one beautiful package so that clients could choose the space that was best for their wedding. Jenn and Daniel chose a painted wood bench beneath a leafy oak tree.

As they unwrapped their sandwiches, Jenn said, "I'd love to hear more about your career as a photojournalist."

"I mostly shot photographs for newspaper and magazine articles focusing on social issues. I tried to cover areas that people seemed to want to ignore or write off as beyond help. I also did some war reporting in South Sudan and Iraq."

"That sounds dangerous."

"It was, but I had security around me in the truly

dangerous situations, whereas the people I photographed in those war-torn countries didn't have that kind of protection. And the truth is that some of the things I photographed in other 'safer' situations have felt almost as dangerous."

Jenn's eyebrows knotted together. "What do you mean?"

"Not everyone wants their story told with pictures," he explained. "I've upset plenty of businessmen and a gang member or two." Daniel would never forget the times he'd had to run, or shoot his pictures from a hiding spot, or take them with gunfire sounding close by. "At the time, it all seemed rather exciting, but after Victoria died, I needed to make sure I could be here for the kids. I was also ready to tell happier stories by then—where I would know for sure that everything had turned out okay in the end."

"Is that how you got into wedding photography?"

Nodding, he said, "I know most photographers do weddings and events to pay the bills until they can make their name with more 'serious' work. But the way I look at it is that weddings are one of the biggest events in people's lives. The photos I take at a wedding might not matter to everyone else in the world, but to the bride and groom, they mean everything."

"I love the way you just put that," she said with a smile that mesmerized him.

Happy to be sitting with her in the shade of the leafy tree with the warm sea air blowing over them, he said, "What about you? How did you get into baking?"

"For years, I'd tried different things. Different jobs. Different hobbies. I even started writing a novel once. Let's just say that I won't be competing with Jason for a spot on the bestseller lists any time soon," she said with a laugh. "But the day I started baking...I *knew* it was right."

"That's how photography was for me."

She gave him another small smile, but it fell away too soon. "Unfortunately, my ex-husband wasn't exactly thrilled with my new passion."

"What was it with him?" Daniel knew he wasn't doing a good job of keeping his irritation with her ex out of his voice, but he simply couldn't help it. The guy really made him mad.

"He doesn't think baked goods are healthy. He didn't want them in the house—didn't even like smelling them baking in the kitchen."

"Now I know for sure that the guy is nuts. Everyone knows one of the best things in the world is walking into a kitchen that smells like a fresh-baked cake or cookies." But that wasn't nearly enough. Jenn deserved to know what a wonderful person she was, needed to know there were people out there who thought far more of her than her husband obviously had. People like Daniel. "Your baking is amazing, Jenn. *You're* amazing."

Her eyes went wide, and her cheeks flushed. "Thank you." He was wondering if he should say—or do—something more, when she suddenly added, "You've got something on your shirt." She reached out and brushed several crumbs away, then looked up abruptly, as though she'd just overstepped her bounds. "Sorry."

"Don't be sorry." He loved that she'd instinctively done something so sweet and intimate. But at the same time, he knew better than to make a big deal out of it. "Someone has got to make sure I don't scare off potential clients by showing up to a meeting wearing lunch."

Fortunately, the moment of tension disappeared when she smiled back. They were just heading back into the kitchen when Daniel got a return call from the folks over at *Brides* magazine. She continued inside while he remained in the gardens so that he wouldn't distract her while he talked on the phone.

After he quickly explained how he and Jenn had been working together to document the baking process each step of the way, the editor said, "We don't usually use photographers who aren't on our books. Then again, we never thought we'd be working with Daniel Brooker, either. We're all big fans of your work here."

Glad that his reputation might help with this project, he spent a few minutes going over technical details with the editor. "Everyone at Married in Malibu is intent on making sure the shoot goes as smoothly as possible," he assured her before they hung up.

By the time he made it back to the kitchen, Jenn was mapping out the elements she would need to construct the castle of the theme-park cake. Honestly, it looked more like a feat of engineering than baking.

When his phone rang again, he wondered if the *Brides* editor was calling back with additional instructions. But it was Kayla.

"Hey, sweetie. What's up?"

"You haven't forgotten about tonight, have you, Dad?"

They were going to the movies. "Of course I haven't forgotten. You, me, and Adam at a *Frozen* sing-along."

"What about Jenn? Can she come too?"

When he looked over at Jenn and saw that she was smiling at him, he figured there was no time like the present to make his next move. Plus, he did like to encourage his daughter's great ideas.

"Kayla would like to know if you can go to a *Frozen* sing-along with us tonight." He needed her to know that Kayla wasn't the only one who wanted her to come along. "I'd like to know too."

Fortunately, instead of looking ambushed by him and his daughter, Jenn only smiled wider. "I'd love to."

Chapter Ten

Jenn couldn't believe how difficult it was to get ready to go to the movies with Daniel and his kids.

"Not special enough," she said, rejecting her favorite pair of dark jeans. She didn't want to look the way she looked at work every day, because that would imply that this was no big deal. But when she held up a sleek black dress and looked at herself in the mirror, that didn't feel right either. She'd bought it to remind herself that she could be sexy if she wanted to be, regardless of everything Oliver had said—but a sing-along animated movie was definitely not the time for a little black dress.

"There has to be *something*." A moment later, she spotted it. A light blue fitted sweater worn with a dark skirt with light blue embroidery at the hem. It had a bit of color and prettiness without being over the top.

There wasn't enough time by then to do more than put on a touch of lipstick and a little eye shadow. On impulse, before she left her bedroom, she rooted through her jewelry box for her sparkling crystal earrings cut in the shape of miniature cupcakes. She loved how the crystals caught the light with every movement she made. She was tying her hair into a loose ponytail when her doorbell rang.

When she opened the door, she found herself met by a sudden storm of hugs. Kayla squeezed Jenn around the waist, while Adam managed to grab one of her legs, almost knocking her over with the force of his affection.

"It's great to see you both too." She looked at their father standing behind them. "Hi, Daniel."

He seemed to take in her hair and makeup and outfit in a split second, and she could have sworn there was admiration—and more than a little heat—in his gaze. "You look great, Jenn."

"Oh wow, your earrings are *amazing*," Kayla said.

Before Jenn could thank Daniel's daughter for the compliment, Adam asked, "Do you have cakes all over your house?"

"I mostly leave the cakes at work," Jenn replied. "But fortunately there should be plenty to choose from at the Cheesecake Factory."

"It's our favorite place to eat ever," Kayla said. "We love their pizza too."

"And then after dinner," Adam added, "we get to sing, *Let it go, let it g—*"

"How about we wait until we're there, Adam?" Daniel said. He was smiling, despite the fact that he'd likely heard the kids sing the popular song a hundred times by now. He glanced down at his watch. "We should get moving, or there won't be enough time to have dinner before the movie starts."

Daniel and Jenn found themselves alone on the sidewalk when the kids ran to get back in the car. "I hope Kayla and Adam aren't too overwhelming."

"They're great," Jenn assured him. "Trust me, you don't ever have to apologize for your kids."

"You're only saying that because neither of them has spilled bright-colored juice on anything expensive yet."

"Given the amount of colored frosting I get on my clothes, I think most of what I own is pretty spill resistant."

Standing together on the sidewalk chatting about his kids shouldn't have been a big deal. Especially considering that they spent hours together at work talking about similar subjects. But she couldn't deny that the moment felt strangely electric, as exciting as if it were a first date with a guy she'd been crushing on.

Only, it wasn't a date, was it? It was just an impromptu trip to dinner and a movie with a co-worker and his kids. Which, she reminded herself, should be more than enough for the time being considering she wasn't one hundred percent sure that she was even up to a new relationship.

She wanted so badly to be sure. But just like Tamara

had said during their chat in the café, if they proved that they had good chemistry while working on the *Brides* spread, then maybe that would mean they would be okay taking things to the next level.

The drive to the restaurant was quieter than Jenn had anticipated. She'd expected a string of questions from the kids and had been looking forward to asking them questions about school and sports and their favorite hobbies. Instead, they spent the journey whispering in the backseat together.

"What are you two plotting back there?" Daniel finally asked.

"Nothing, Dad," they said in unison.

Clearly, they were up to something, but by then they were parking in front of the restaurant and the kids were unbuckling and rushing inside to check in for a table. Kayla and Adam ended up choosing seats on the same side of the table, leaving Jenn and Daniel to sit next to each other on the opposite side.

It wasn't much of a leap to guess what the kids had been whispering about in the car. To think that they might want to make a match between Jenn and their father was very sweet.

Dinner was every bit as loud and chaotic and fun as Jenn had hoped it would be. Especially when Kayla asked her father to tell them about his travels around the world.

"It must have been exciting to experience so many new things," Jenn mused.

"There definitely were great moments, but while Niagara Falls and Baffin Island will still be there a year from now, I didn't want to miss Kayla taking her first steps or Adam's first tooth falling out any more than I wanted to miss the Saturday afternoon soccer games or cupcake-baking marathons."

Everything Daniel had described—simple family life and a warm house full of laughter—used to be her dream. But somewhere along the way, she'd stopped fantasizing about it when she'd realized Oliver didn't share the same dream.

She had assumed the dream had died completely for her. But had it been lying in wait all this time for the right person to come along? Someone who knew exactly how to make that dream a reality?

They had cheesecake after the main meal, of course. Kayla laughed while she demolished a slice with whole Oreos embedded in it, while Adam had the peanut butter fudge ripple cup cheesecake. Oh yes, her ex definitely had no idea what he was missing out on...

"So," Daniel said when they were finished, "who's ready to sing?"

"Me!" Kayla and Adam said at the same time.

"What about you, Jenn?"

"I am too." A sing-along movie wasn't something

she normally did, but she was looking forward to it. And
when Daniel bought a family ticket for the four of them,
warmth spread through her. Because even if she wasn't
sure yet that she was emotionally ready for a new
relationship—especially one that came with the respon-
sibilities of two young children—it was undeniably fun
to be a part of their tight unit for one night.

It wasn't until they reached their seats that she realized they had been set up again by the kids. This time,
they were bookended with Kayla on Jenn's left and
Adam on Daniel's right.

Jenn had never seen *Frozen* before, which made her
the odd one out in a movie theater packed with families
who knew every single word and were even dressed in
costumes. Honestly, though, there was nowhere Jenn
would rather have been—especially when Daniel started
singing in a warm baritone. And when she made a stab
at singing along with a couple of songs with repeating
choruses, the pleased look he gave her made her feel as
good as if she'd just won *Cupcake Wars*.

It was over far too soon. She couldn't remember the
last time she'd had this much fun. She didn't want the
night to end.

"What now?" Kayla asked, obviously feeling the
same way. She had grabbed Jenn's hand while they were
walking out of the theater and hadn't let go.

"Now it's time to get you two home and into bed,"
Daniel replied. Before the kids could protest, he added,

"And since Jenn has been working so hard all week, we should probably take her home to get some rest after wearing out her vocal cords tonight."

It was true, everyone seemed tired as they drove back. Parking a few houses away, they all got out to walk Jenn to her door.

"I had such a great time tonight," Jenn told them. "Thank you for inviting me."

Kayla and Adam responded with hugs that were even tighter than the ones they'd given her earlier when they'd arrived to pick her up. Jenn hugged them back just as tight.

Daniel pulled his phone out, obviously intending to capture the moment with a photo. Before Jenn realized what Kayla was doing, she had pulled the three of them close enough to her father to include him in the group hug.

It felt so much like they were a family right then that it was almost impossible for Jenn to keep the tears out of her eyes.

"Time to go, kids," Daniel finally said, although he didn't sound like he wanted to break away from the hug any more than she did.

As the three of them walked back to their car and Jenn stood on her doorstep watching them pile into the minivan, she couldn't help but wish that she could go with them to their home full of warmth and laughter.

And, most important of all, love.

Chapter Eleven

The next day was a rare Saturday with no wedding, which meant that Jenn was the only person at Married in Malibu. For all her progress, there was still so much to do, which was why she was working while everyone else took the day off. Not only finishing up the individual components for the cakes, but also the assembly and decoration. The sugar and marzipan detail work alone was enough to make her start to panic.

"Breathe," Jenn reminded herself. Spiraling off into an anxious mess wasn't going to help. Instead, she simply needed to tackle her list one item at a time—especially the one big thing she'd been avoiding all week that had been hanging over her casting its shadows.

Her ex.

Jenn pulled out her phone where there were several new texts from Oliver. All of them had the same theme: While he acknowledged that things had ended badly, he "really needed" to see her.

She couldn't ignore him any longer, no matter how

much she wished she could. His frequent texts were a huge distraction, especially when she had such a big project to complete. But she was determined to set up a meeting on her terms, not his—in a place where she felt safe and at a time that was convenient for her.

I can see you today, 11 am at Malibu T and Coffee.

Her phone dinged less than five seconds later with his affirmative response. Looked like she was going to be having coffee with her ex today.

Ugh.

Fortunately, for the next few hours, she would be doing her favorite thing in the world: creating beautiful wedding cakes.

She set to work on the decorations for the Malibu-themed cake, and then while her seashells and starfish were setting, she began to frost the traditional cake. By the time she stopped to take a break, she had used nearly a gallon of icing and had made so many caramel shells that she could have restocked the beach with them.

Thankfully, exhilaration had overtaken anxiety while she worked. She truly was the luckiest person in the world to have a job she loved so much—one where she could let her creativity loose every single day, with the knowledge that she was making a bride and groom happy on their special day.

But it wasn't only her job that had her feeling like

she was walking on air. It was Daniel. Every time she thought about him, she couldn't stop smiling.

What a difference a week made. After everything Oliver had done, Jenn had sworn off men. She'd planned to forever cut herself off from emotion, to just focus on her work, and never, ever risk her heart with anyone again. But she couldn't stop thinking about Daniel, couldn't stop dreaming of what it would be like to have his arms wrapped around her, his lips pressed to hers...

Last week, she would have told herself to stop dreaming, to stop wishing. But the more she got to know him, the more she wanted to risk. Risk opening up to him the way he'd opened up to her. Risk showing him everything that lay in her heart.

Just then, the alarm on her phone went off. It was nearly eleven. Time to meet Oliver.

Refusing to let herself be nervous—or to fix her hair or clothes—she washed and dried her hands, took off her apron, then headed over to Tamara's café.

At first glance, she didn't see him. Until she looked closer at a guy in the corner who looked like he might be a monk with his shaved head and kaftan. It was only when he waved that Jenn realized he was Oliver.

"Oliver?"

"Jenn, namaste." Oliver stood to greet her, bowing as he did so. "It's good to see you again. Will you sit down? They do a wonderful herbal infusion here that's great for the mind. Can I get you one?"

Before she could answer, Oliver waved imperiously at Tamara and ordered for Jenn. Thankfully, Tamara knew to make her a latte instead.

"How have you been?" He didn't wait for her to reply. "*I've* had a lot of changes recently. A macrobiotic diet is so much healthier than polluting one's body with junk, and it's helped me so much in my yoga practice. I'm sure you won't be surprised to hear that I've been focusing on Ashtanga recently."

Oliver always assumed that everyone around him was interested in every detail of his life, but right then, Jenn was glad. It meant she had some time to figure out how she wanted to deal with him while he went into a story about meeting Sting in the middle of a yoga session.

"...he was so flexible, you wouldn't believe it. Really something to aspire to, except of course, aspiration is born out of envy, and we should all learn to put it aside..."

Oliver was good at filling space with whatever thoughts came into his head. He quickly drifted from yoga and onto the incredible mileage his hybrid car got. Subjects sped past: his solar heating system, the brilliant business idea he'd had while sitting in meditation watching the sunset.

As he continued in one seemingly continuous stream

of thought, she wondered if he had mastered some kind of yoga technique that let him keep talking without taking a breath. Then again, speaking without giving her a chance to respond was something he'd always done.

"...and that's when I realized that living meant living in harmony with the world so that..."

Tamara brought over her coffee, major questions in her eyes. She wasn't the only one wondering what was going on here.

"Oliver." Jenn said his name firmly enough that he couldn't ignore her. "I'm glad to hear that you're doing well, but like I said in my text, I have a lot of work to do. So as fascinating as this all is, I would appreciate it if you could tell me why you wanted to meet. Presumably, it was for more than just letting me know you'd met Sting."

Oliver looked a little taken aback. And no wonder, given that during their time together, he'd been in control of things. He opened and closed his mouth a couple of times, looking like a particularly well-toned goldfish.

Finally, he recovered himself. "You sound like you could really benefit from the yoga and meditation retreat I recently went to. We learned to let stress go and forget about time constraints. Booking a week for yourself might help."

A laugh escaped her before she could stop it. There

had been a time when she would have wanted to throw her coffee at him, but strangely, none of his little barbs hurt. Instead, she felt as though she was having coffee with a cartoon character. "Well, if that's all you needed to tell me, I've got to get back to work."

She was just about to push back from the table, when he said, "Jenn, no! Don't leave yet."

It was the genuine panic in his voice that had her staying where she was.

"I came to say I'm sorry for anything I might have done to hurt you."

Jenn was speechless for a long moment. Not because he'd apologized—which was a major rarity. But because of *how* he'd apologized.

Anything he *might* have done? It was as if he couldn't possibly figure out why she was upset. Like, say, because he'd cheated on her. Or, perhaps, because he'd lied to her.

She nearly did throw her coffee at him this time. Because underneath his veneer of calm and spirituality, he was still the same man. Empty and vain.

She hated that she'd fallen for his act all those years ago. Hated that she'd been so foolish. Hated that she'd been so desperate for love that she'd thought he loved her, when the truth was that Oliver would never love anyone but himself.

Refusing to even address his faux apology, she said,

"We've gone our separate ways, and it has worked out for the best for both of us. It sounds like you have some interesting things going on in your life right now, and I hope you have great success and happiness with whatever you do next. Now, if you'll excuse me, I need to go."

She stood up quickly, intent on getting out of there as quickly as possible. She wanted nothing more than to shake off this meeting, just shove it out of her heart and mind completely.

"Jenn, wait!" Oliver's hand clamped down on her arm.

Tamara stepped out from behind the counter, obviously looking to intervene, but Jenn gave her friend a small shake of her head. As good as it was of her friend to look out for her, Jenn needed to be the one to deal with this.

"Let go of me, Oliver."

He did, thankfully, but he kept talking. "There are still so many things I haven't told you. Things haven't worked out very well with Varla." Varla was the woman she'd caught him in bed with. "We're calling it quits. I've done a lot of soul-searching these past few weeks, and I've come to realize that I made a terrible mistake. I almost can't forgive myself, but I think we can agree that everyone deserves a second chance. I've meditated on this a lot. I've consulted my guru. I even asked Sting what he thought when we ran into each other in the yoga session." He paused. Dramatically. "I love you, Jenn. I've always loved you, and I want to get back together. We were so good together, and I want that again."

There was a time when she would have killed to hear those words. In the months after their marriage had fallen apart, she had wanted nothing more than for Oliver to come crawling back, telling her how wrong he'd been, and promising to do anything to make it up to her.

Now, though, it wasn't enough. It couldn't be enough when she'd finally realized that the man she'd thought she'd fallen in love with had been nothing more than a figment of her imagination.

"Oliver—"

"I know baking is important to you, and I want you to know that you can have sugar in the house."

Her mouth fell open. "You're willing to *let* me have sugar in the house?"

"I am," he said, as if he'd just conceded absolutely everything to her. As if he was doing her the biggest favor in the world by even sitting here with her. "In fact, not only am I ready to give us another shot, I have everything mapped out. We should create an exclusive retreat catering to the physical and spiritual needs of only the most select clients. You could oversee all the cooking. Of course, you will have to learn to cook healthy food, but I'm sure that with enough dedication you could come up to speed fairly quickly. And, of course, you would want to keep your position at the wedding company for a long as possible. I mean, just think of the connections you must be making there with all those stars."

Aha. At long last, they'd gotten to the heart of what Oliver wanted: Her connections to the rich and famous.

He wasn't sorry about anything. He didn't truly want to get back together. But he *did* want a fast track to fortune and fame for himself.

There were at least a dozen different things she could have said about how selfish he was, how manipulative, how condescending. But he wasn't worth the breath it would take to say them. And he definitely wasn't worth another minute away from her cakes.

"Good-bye, Oliver."

She made a beeline for the door, but before she could get away, he leaped in front of her. "At least think about everything I'm offering, Jenn. I *need* this." He quickly added, "And you. I need you too."

The next thing she knew, he was hugging her. And, for a few moments, she was so stunned that she didn't push him away.

Chapter Twelve

Jenn was the first person Daniel thought about when he woke up on Saturday. No surprise, given that he'd spent the entire drive back from the movie the previous night fighting to keep his eyes on the road. She was that wonderful, that beautiful, that fun. He didn't normally come into work on a free Saturday, but after the kids won both their soccer games that morning, he'd been unable to stay away, knowing that she would be there.

When he'd told the kids that he was going in to work, Kayla had looked at Adam and said, "He's going so he can see Jenn."

"Yes!" Adam had high-fived his sister.

"We've got a really big project going right now," Daniel had explained with a laugh. Of course, it had been really good to see just how much his kids liked Jenn.

And then, when he'd driven them over to his parents for the afternoon, his mother had said, "They work you far too hard. Don't get me wrong, I'm thrilled that you're no longer traveling around the world being shot at. But I can't imagine what's so interesting that it has you going in there on a weekend when there isn't even a wedding."

Daniel had deliberately not looked at his kids' giggly faces when his mother said that. If his parents got wind of Jenn, they'd probably go to Married in Malibu to beg her to go out with him. While her going out with him was exactly the result he wanted, he hoped he could pull it off without his mother intervening on his behalf.

"I'm working on a photo spread in a major magazine," was the only explanation he'd given. "I really appreciate you stepping in with the kids today."

"Well, this is obviously very important to you. But you've had plenty of spreads in magazines, so the moment you get back I'm expecting you to tell me what this is *really* about." The kids had giggled even harder at that. They loved it when his mother talked to Daniel like he was their age.

Fifteen minutes later, he'd been happy to see that Jenn's car was the only one in the Married in Malibu lot. He'd been tempted to dash straight into the kitchen to see her, but he liked surprising her with coffee and a pastry. So he had set off across the street to Malibu T & Coffee, more determined than ever to win her heart, whatever it took.

"Hi, Tamara," Daniel said once he stepped inside the

café. "One latte and one Americano, please."

He was normally more talkative, but just then he was trying to come up with the perfect place to take Jenn to dinner. No kids this time, just the two of them. He wanted to sweep her off her feet so completely that there would be no doubt anymore about what was between them. Somewhere with candles and soft music and—

Wait a minute. Why was a man in a kaftan hugging Jenn in the corner? Especially when she looked so unhappy about it?

"Hey!" Daniel called out. "What do you think you're doing, buddy? Get your hands off her."

The bald man was surprisingly large and looked menacing as he drew back from Jenn with an irritated scowl. Daniel might have been intimidated if he hadn't once spent an afternoon in a bunker taking photographs while bombs had gone off so close by that the ground shook.

"What Jenn and I do is none of your business," the man said, trying his best to loom over Daniel. "And I should warn you that the branch of Buddhist meditation I practice has *strong* links to the Shaolin Monastery."

"That's enough, Oliver," Jenn said.

"Oliver?" This was Oliver? The scumbag who had treated Jenn so badly? Who had cheated on her, then left her to pick up the pieces of her life in his wake?

"Daniel," Jenn said, "I'm glad you're here. I was just heading back to the office."

Before Daniel could respond, Oliver stepped between them. "I'd appreciate it if you could leave me to continue this very important conversation I'm having with my wife—"

"Your *ex*-wife," Daniel growled.

"—about our future together."

Future together? Was this guy on something? There was no way that Jenn would ever go back to someone who had hurt her the way her ex-husband had.

"Oliver," she said with a sigh, "I've already told you there's no future for us."

"Baby," he crooned in the smarmiest way possible, "I know my offer to get back together with you is more than you ever expected, but I have faith that you'll see the light soon."

Daniel was tempted to shove the guy away from her, but even as furious as he was at her ex, he knew she wouldn't be impressed by his brawling over her like some high school kid. Still, he took a step toward Oliver and said in a low voice, "Jenn has made herself clear. It's time for you to leave."

"How do you know anything about what my Jenn wants?"

"She's not *your* anything," Daniel snapped back. Everything about this guy was wrong for Jenn. It was hard to believe that he had ever meant anything to her, let alone been her husband.

"Oh, I see," Oliver said suddenly, his eyes narrowed. "You're here playing the big man because you want Jenn for yourself, don't you?" He poked at Daniel's chest. "Too bad, because she's always been mine and still is."

"Are you kidding me?" How could this man talk about Jenn like she was some sort of possession, rather than someone to be loved? "After what you did to her, do you really think she still wants to be with you?"

"Please," Jenn said to both of them. "Please stop this."

"Why?" Oliver's kaftan flapped around him as he spun back to face her. "So that you can go running off with *Daniel*? I have a brilliant future mapped out for us. Do you think I'm going to throw all that away just because some guy wants to get you into bed?"

Daniel couldn't stop himself from grabbing Oliver by the shoulders. "I care about Jenn."

"Care about her?" Oliver snorted. "You want her. You want to put your grubby hands all over her and make her yours. You're a parasite moving in where you're not wanted. A scavenger. Well, I was here first. I was Jenn's first, her one, her only. You can't take that away, no matter how hard you try. She's mine. She always was, and she always will be."

Daniel had been determined not to sink to Oliver's

level. The smart thing to do would be to walk away from the argument. Be the bigger man.

But he couldn't do it. Not when he needed to defend Jenn against this *idiot*.

"The fact that you think Jenn could ever be yours again shows how little you deserve to be with her. Do you even see her? Do you see how happy she is without you? Do you even know, do you even care, what she wants from her life? Because I know for sure that Jenn loves baking and you never supported her in a single moment of it." Daniel knew his voice was loud enough for everyone in the café to hear, but he wasn't done ripping into her ex yet. "You had years to see what an amazing, beautiful person she is, but instead you spent all your time trying to change her. Cheating on her." His hands tightened into fists as he spoke. It would feel so good to connect with the other man's jaw and see him go down. To punish him for what he had done. If anyone deserved it, Oliver did. "You must be a truly awful person to hurt someone so sweet."

Oliver was just about to launch his right fist into Daniel's face when Tamara called out, "Hey, no fighting in my shop!"

But Oliver had no intention of stopping. And Daniel was glad for the chance to grab the other man's hand out of thin air and push him back against the counter.

"Jenn and I are special," Oliver insisted as he tried to

break Daniel's grip.

But Daniel had had much bigger, stronger men try to intimidate him. He wasn't going to let Oliver win. "You don't deserve her in your life for another minute. You spent your entire marriage ignoring her and treating her like dirt. You didn't deserve the time that you had with her, and you certainly don't deserve to have any more now. Do everyone a favor, Oliver. Go away and don't come back."

"Enough," Tamara said, pushing her way between them.

"Spoilsport," said an older woman who had been watching the show with relish. "We haven't even gotten to see a good fight yet."

"And you're not going to," Tamara said, holding the two men at arm's length. She nodded to Oliver. "You need to leave." She pinned Daniel with nearly as hard of a look. "Daniel, sit down."

"You can't—" Oliver began.

"If you have a problem with it, I suggest you meditate on it," Tamara said with bite. "Now get the hell out of my coffee shop."

Oliver swept away with what he probably thought was Zen-like calm, though it came off as petulance.

"Good riddance," Daniel said.

Tamara lifted a warning finger. "I told you to sit down."

Daniel recognized that voice. It was one he occasionally used with his kids when they'd behaved particularly badly. He took a seat.

"Now," Tamara said, "take a look around my coffee shop and tell me what's missing."

Daniel turned to scan the café. "Jenn's gone."

"Exactly." Tamara put a hand on his shoulder when he tried to stand. "You're not going anywhere until you understand what an idiot you've just been."

"But I—"

Tamara's look was, yet again, one that he might give his kids at their most belligerent. "She left here in tears. Ran off while you were trying to go ten rounds with Mr. New Age."

"I didn't know," Daniel said.

"No, you didn't. Because you weren't watching her. Because you weren't even thinking about her."

"That's not true. I never wanted to hurt her."

He would have done anything rather than upset her. Obviously, his expression said as much, because Tamara sighed.

"I know you didn't. You wanted to defend her honor. You probably even thought that you were doing the right thing. But what just went down with her ex? Don't try to pretend that it was about Jenn." She shook her head at him. "That was about the two of you trying to prove who was the bigger man. When it only made both of you look like fools."

"I thought they looked pretty good," the gray-haired woman offered from a table in the corner. Both Tamara and Daniel ignored her.

"Don't get me wrong," Tamara continued. "That ex-husband of hers needed handling. But *Jenn* had handled him. She'd already told him to take a hike when you showed up and barged into the middle of it."

"I didn't mean to screw everything up. I just wanted—"

"Her. You wanted her. You were fighting over her like some kind of prize—instead of showing her how much you care about her. You should have been by her side no matter what. Instead, you didn't even notice when she left."

Daniel couldn't believe how badly he'd blown it, all because he'd been caught up in the challenge of besting her ex. "I need to make this up to her."

"You sure do. You need to apologize. You need to grovel. You need to ask her what's in her heart and then really listen to what she says." Tamara paused before adding, "And you need to tell her you love her."

Chapter Thirteen

For once, Jenn didn't head to the kitchen. Normally, whipping up a batch of decadent muffins or individually piping profiteroles drove away the pain. But her hands were shaking too badly right now to go anywhere near her cakes. If she tried to add the finishing touches for the *Brides* shoot now, she would just bring everything crashing down around her. Plus, she knew Daniel would come to the kitchen to find her, and she wasn't ready to face him. Not yet.

Feeling numb, yet wired at the same time, she headed down to the beach. The cove in front of Married in Malibu was empty as always. The ocean lapped against the shore, blue and foaming with breakers. The sand reflected the warm sunshine above. And she was truly alone with her thoughts.

Right then, however, she didn't know if that was a good thing or not.

"Why does it have to be so hard?"

No answer came from the ocean, or the birds in the

sky, or the shells scattered along the sand. As much as she wished for it, there was no carefully constructed recipe that would tell her everything she needed to feel. Not only about Oliver, but also about Daniel.

Everything had been going so well. Their outing with the kids had been fantastic, and she'd been sure that there would soon be more than that. But now that she'd ended up in the middle of a chest-beating competition between Daniel and Oliver...it felt as though everything had gone back to square one.

Not only with any potential romantic relationships, but also with her job. Soon, she knew, everyone at Married in Malibu would find out what had happened in the coffee shop. She was supposed to be an essential component of Married in Malibu's growth, not get caught up in arguments with her ex-husband in the café across the street. If anyone had recorded the awful scene on their phone and recognized Jenn and Daniel as Married in Malibu employees, the wedding venue could end up getting the wrong kind of publicity.

Liz had given her the biggest chance of her life. The opportunity to put her past behind her and move on. Only to have Jenn betray that trust by dragging her old life into the picture.

It was impossible not to feel sick about the whole thing. Even the sight of the ocean in front of her wasn't working to clear away the anxious thoughts buzzing around in her head.

"Jenn?"

At the sound of Daniel's voice, she turned to see him standing on the sand, looking a little disheveled but unhurt. She hated the thought that he and Oliver might have had a fistfight over her.

"I'm sorry."

His apology—with none of the excuses Oliver would have led with—touched her deep in the middle of her chest.

"I know you might not be ready to accept my apology yet," he said softly when she remained silent, "but I needed to make sure you were okay."

Once upon a time, she would have automatically said that she was fine, because she wouldn't have wanted to make Daniel any more uncomfortable than he already was. But she wasn't that woman anymore. Wasn't a woman who could pretend to feel something she didn't just to make someone else happy. Because that had never worked, had it? Not for her or anyone else.

"I'm not okay. Seeing you two behave like that in Tamara's coffee shop was embarrassing, and scary, and overwhelming. I wish it never happened."

"You're right," he said in a somber tone. "It's just that when I saw him harassing you…" He swallowed hard. "I wanted to protect you. Instead, I let myself get drawn into an argument when I should have been focusing on you." Daniel looked ashamed in a way that Oliver never would have. Her ex not only wouldn't have understood what the problem was, he likely wouldn't have understood that there was a problem in the first place. "I should have been supporting you, should have trusted you to have the situation well in hand."

She'd been so mortified when the argument broke out. She'd felt like a spectator in her own life, forced into the background while Daniel and Oliver argued over her in front of Tamara's customers. Even thinking about it brought back the shame of her private life being picked apart in public.

She wanted to let herself sink into Daniel's arms. To just hold onto him until everything was better. Instead, she sank down on the sand, wrapped her arms around her knees, and admitted, "I didn't have the situation in hand. Not really. Not when he grabbed me. I should have been tougher with him. I shouldn't have met with him in the first place. But he seemed so desperate to meet that I didn't know what else to do."

Daniel sat down beside her on the sand. At any other time, it would have been a beautiful moment—the two of them on the beach, looking out over the ocean. But this wasn't one of the perfect, romantic moments that Daniel captured with his camera at a wedding. This was real, messy, painful life.

"I know what it's like to rebuild your life after things

have gone wrong," he said in a gentle voice. "I know how hard it can shake you when you see a reminder of the past for the first time. But you deserve so much better than Oliver. That's what makes me so angry. He had someone as wonderful as you in his life and he didn't see it. He didn't see how important you should have been to him. How perfect you are."

"I'm not perfect." She spoke so softly that her words could barely be heard above the surf. "I'm like everyone else. Maybe not even as together as that, because a normal person wouldn't have just thrown away her future in a coffee shop."

"You haven't thrown away anything."

"After I brought my personal life into work like this? If I just generated negative publicity for Married in Malibu, I'll be lucky if Liz doesn't fire me."

"She won't do that," Daniel said. "I'll explain to her what happened—"

"This is my life coming apart at the seams. My problems. I need to be the one to sort them out," she insisted. "By myself."

"You don't have to do it alone, Jenn. Not anymore." He reached out to touch her cheek, gently turning her head toward him so that she could see the certainty, the sincerity in his eyes. "I love you. I want to protect you and support you, hold you and be there for you, whatever happens."

His declaration should have been a revelation, a ray of light. Instead, Jenn found herself struggling to take it in, especially coming so soon after what just happened with Oliver.

"You're so sweet," she finally said, turning her face so that his hand fell away from her skin. "Too sweet."

"Jenn." She could hear the emotion in his voice as he said her name. The frustration that she hadn't leaped at his declaration...and also that she wasn't saying the three little words back to him. "I didn't say it to be sweet. I said it because it's what I feel. What I've always felt for you from the first moment we met, the first moment we spoke, the first time I ever saw you smile, the first time you laughed—and it felt like everything was right with the world."

She couldn't believe all the wonderful things he was saying. Couldn't believe an amazing man like him was saying them to *her*.

"You're wonderful, Daniel." And yet, she still needed him to understand why she wasn't jumping at being with him. Needed him to know that it had nothing to do with him...and everything to do with her.

"Then be with me."

He made it sound so simple, but she knew better. "My life is so messy. Seeing Oliver again reminded me of just what a mess it still is." The blue of the ocean and the gold of the sand reminded her of Daniel's kids with their blond hair and bright blue eyes. "I know how much you love your kids, and I would never want to do something that would taint what you have with them. I mean, look at me now—you've just said you want to be with me, that you love me. And all I can do is wonder if I'm so wrecked by my bad marriage, by the ugliness of my divorce, that I'll always be waiting for the moment when things start to fall apart."

Daniel had remained quiet, listening in a way that Oliver never would have. Finally, he spoke again. "I'm not going to tell you what to feel, or what to think. You've had enough of that to last a lifetime. But I'll say this: You are not wrecked. You may not be perfect—no one is—but you're still perfect to *me*."

He took her hands in his, and she marveled at the way his large hands fit hers so well. His hands were callused from the time he'd spent in war zones, hers were scarred from her many kitchen mishaps, and yet both were still strong and capable.

"I love you." He held her gaze, not letting her look away. "*I love you.* I never thought I would say that to anyone else after Victoria died. I thought I was the wrecked one, but with you I finally know that second chances really are possible."

Jenn wished that she could say it as easily as he did. She wished she could erase her past and come to him brand new, not only with open arms, but without any fears of failing again.

"You don't have to say anything now." He stroked his fingers over hers, and she felt his touch all the way down deep in the dark places she'd thought could never find the light again. "You don't have to say anything at all if you don't love me too. But I think you do." His lips curved into a smile as he lifted her hands and pressed a kiss to them. "I *know* you do. So I'm prepared to wait for you as long as you need."

Oliver would have pressed on until he got what he wanted, until Jenn said whatever he wanted her to say. But Daniel simply squeezed her hands one last time, then left her to try to untangle her web of thoughts and fears and hopes and dreams while the Malibu waves lapped at her toes.

Chapter Fourteen

The breeze had turned cool by the time Jenn finally headed home. She was so tempted to drive to Daniel's house to ask Adam and Kayla about their soccer games, to make dinner with them, and then sit close enough to Daniel at the dining table that she could feel his leg warm and strong against hers.

But was that just a dream?

Or could it be a reality? What if she reached for happiness and it didn't work? What if she left not only Daniel upset and confused, but also two innocent children?

Endless questions were spinning around and around inside her head when she walked into her apartment building and got the second-biggest shock of her life. The first had been hearing Daniel say, *I love you.*

The second was seeing Oliver in the hall outside her apartment.

"What are you doing here?"

"One of your neighbors let me in." He sat in what

she assumed was the lotus position, his hands on his knees in the classic meditative pose. "I told them that I'm your husband and that you were expecting me."

"You're *not* my husband." She practically yelled the words at him. "You're my *ex*-husband."

Oliver waved that away as he rose to his feet. "Semantics."

Actually, it was a very important distinction. One she obviously needed to make clear to her neighbors so that they wouldn't again make the mistake of letting Oliver into the building to ambush her.

Deciding there was no point in prolonging that argument with him at present, however, she said, "You still haven't answered my question about why you're here."

"We weren't done with our conversation."

"Yes, we were. But you still decided you'd talk your way into my building like some kind of stalker."

She should have seen this coming. Whenever Oliver wanted something, he went after it with a laser focus. In fact, the reason they'd gotten serious in the first place was because he'd been relentless in wooing her, sweeping her off her feet in a whirlwind of romantic gestures. Only now could she finally see that his effort had less to do with him wanting her and more to do with not wanting to fail.

"I'm making a real effort for you here, Jenn." He

looked genuinely hurt. "The least you could do is invite me in so that we can talk things through like two reasonable people."

While a part of her would have liked to have their final showdown in private versus the all-too-public argument in Tamara's café, the fact was that she didn't know Oliver anymore. Didn't know if he might be so close to the edge that he'd act out with her. Going to a semi-private space with lots of facing windows to the apartments that surrounded it, was a much better idea.

"We can talk in the garden." She led him through the outdoor space. "But don't get too comfortable there. You won't be staying long."

In the garden, he sat down on a stone bench, carefully arranging his kaftan around himself. "Once we're running the retreat together, you won't need to live here by yourself anymore. I'll be glad to move in with you so that we'll have more money for capital expenses."

A shocked laugh escaped her throat. Had he truly not heard anything she'd said to him that morning? "I've already told you a partnership isn't going to happen."

"Yes, I know," he said with another of those annoying hand waves meant to minimize her objections. "But that's only because that idiot who thinks he's in love with you showed up before I could tell you why you're wrong to even think of hesitating on this."

Refusing to let him draw her into talking about Daniel, she said, "I'm not hesitating. I don't want to be involved. Period."

"But you haven't listened to a word I have to say." He looked like a petulant child. "Honestly, Jenn, if we're going to make this work, you really need to start understanding some of my needs."

"Like your need to sleep with other people?"

"Exactly. You're acting like I did this huge, unforgivable thing, but even when I explained to you how it was a natural progression of our marriage into something more experimental and exciting, you wouldn't listen. In fact, if we're being totally honest here, I don't think you ever really listened to me during our marriage."

Once upon a time she would have been breaking down. Crying, or shouting, or running away to escape him. Now, all she felt was a solid determination to be done with him once and for all.

"I'm actually glad you're here," she said. "Because it turns out that there are some things I need to say to you."

It was a mark of just how self-deluded he was that he said, "There's no need to apologize for your behavior, Jenn. I'm big enough to understand that you're still growing into the person you need to be."

The contrast between Daniel and Oliver couldn't have been clearer than in that moment. When Daniel had come to the beach after the scene in the café, it had been to apologize and lay his honest feelings on the line. In contrast, Oliver couldn't even be honest with himself. Daniel had been there to make sure that Jenn was all right, but Oliver was here solely to make sure that he got everything he wanted. Daniel was prepared to wait as long as it took for Jenn to be sure about her feelings, while Oliver would do whatever it took to convince Jenn that his feelings were the right ones for her to have too.

"I was angry with you for a long time," she began.

"I already told you that I forgive you, so we can get past that now and—"

Jenn stopped him with a look. She hadn't known that she could do that during their marriage, but now Oliver immediately fell silent. "Don't interrupt me, please." She took a breath to ground herself again. "I was angry, but now I see that you're not worth being angry with. If I get angry with you for being self-centered and inconsiderate, I might as well be angry with the ocean for being wet or the sky for being blue." He was already sputtering with outrage when she added, "The truth is we were never a good fit. I shouldn't have stayed with you as long as I did. I kept expecting you to change, when I knew deep down inside that it was never going to happen."

"So now you're back to blaming me."

"I don't blame you for all of it, even if you did cheat on me. Even if you have never once apologized or even suggested that you might have done something wrong." Was that a flash of shame in his eyes? *Good.* "When I was with you, I didn't know myself very well. I didn't know what I wanted out of life, so I was willing to believe what I wanted was you. And that what you wanted was good enough for me too."

"I can be what you want," Oliver insisted. "I've spent years improving myself to be the best that I can be. I can teach you how to get there too. We can find nirvana together."

It was painfully obvious he believed, with his carefully toned body, his strict diet, and his spiritual philosophies, that he was well on the way to perfection. But as he sat there in his voluminous outfit in the garden, Jenn could see only a man who was so lacking that he would jump on any bandwagon to try to complete himself.

"For so long," she said, "I had this big hole inside of me that I wanted to fill up. It wasn't fair to think that you were the way to do that."

"Now *Daniel* is the one you want to fill up your empty spaces."

"No." Jenn shook her head firmly. "*I'm* the one who's going to fill my own empty spaces this time around. In fact, I already am."

"Do you really think you're making a difference with your cakes and pies?" He didn't quite sneer, but probably only because it would have added lines to his unnaturally smooth features.

"You know what?" She realized she was smiling. Even in the middle of this horrible—and long overdue—showdown with her ex-husband, her passion for what she did shone through. "I am. Baking is what I'm meant to do. It gave me a way to stand on my own two feet after we split up. It brought me friends and the chance to work somewhere really exciting. And it makes other people happy too. I'm finally becoming the person I've always wanted to be, and I don't need to apologize to you or anyone else for that."

It was the strongest thing she'd ever said to him, even after she'd caught him in bed with another woman. All her emotions at that point had been rooted in how lost she'd thought she'd be without him, how emotionally betrayed she'd felt. Now, however, she finally realized that she was more than strong enough to move forward on her own—and to head in a *great* direction.

By the pinched expression around Oliver's eyes, Jenn knew just how much hearing this truth hurt. "I still think that we can work this out," he said, but this time it sounded more like a plea than a confident statement. "I can see that you're infatuated with this Daniel guy, but—"

"Even if he wasn't in the picture, there's no way I would ever get back together with you. *Ever.*"

"But I thought…" More of his false exterior calm cracked. "I need this, Jenn. I don't know what to do if you don't come back to me."

"Do what I did," Jenn suggested in a far gentler tone than she'd used so far. "Do the best you can and create a new life for yourself. But understand that it's not going to be one that includes me. I don't want to be with you. I don't want anything to do with your business idea. We're done. We've been done for a very long time."

Oliver looked like he was searching inside himself, hoping to find that one argument that would magically turn things around and make Jenn throw herself into his arms. Finally, though, his shoulders slumped.

"I don't know what to say."

"There's nothing left to say. It's over. I wish you the best of luck with the rest of your life, Oliver. But you should go now." *And don't ever come back.*

He seemed so much smaller leaving the garden than he had coming in. Only when she saw his car drive away did she dare to relax.

Oliver was gone.

For good.

She ran a bath to wash away some of the tension from her body. As she sank deep into the hot water, she realized that Oliver was surprisingly easy to let go of. Even so, she couldn't relax completely. Not when she had far more important things—and people—to consider.

Daniel had said that he loved her. Repeatedly, and with such conviction, such honesty, that her heart flipped around inside her chest every time she replayed their conversation in her head. He'd given her the space to make up her mind about what she felt, but she already knew the answer to that.

The only question that remained was whether she had the courage to risk her heart one more time...

Chapter Fifteen

Jenn woke up the next morning profoundly glad that her old feelings about Oliver that had been muddying the waters since their divorce were now gone. She knew now that things never could have worked out between them. There simply wasn't enough overlap between what she and Oliver wanted out of life. In truth, she'd been lucky to get out when she had. And it *had* been good to get everything off her chest—even if she wished they could have skipped the big scene in Tamara's coffee shop.

Speaking of which, she was still worried about Liz's response. Jenn knew she should call her boss to explain, but she wanted to feel clearer, calmer—less over-whelmed—first. Yes, she had plenty of work left to do on her cakes. But it was still too soon to head back into the Married in Malibu kitchen and risk making a mistake.

She spent Sunday reading through her favorite cookbooks, then going to her favorite cookware store and choosing several beautiful new cookie cutters to use on the new cookie recipes she'd decided to put together. By that evening she did feel better, thank you.

Still, by Monday morning, Daniel's *I love you* continued to play over and over in her head, and she was equal parts excited and nervous about seeing him. It wasn't that she didn't trust that his feelings were true, or thought that hers for him were fleeting. She cared for him. Deeply.

But though she'd been brave enough to walk out on her bad marriage, and brave enough to start a new career at Married in Malibu, was she brave enough to open her heart up all the way again? Daniel deserved to be with someone who wouldn't hold anything back from him or his children.

Could she be that woman?

The morning's first test of Jenn's bravery came when Liz walked into Married in Malibu's main building at the same time that she came in through the garden door. Seeing that Liz was holding a Malibu T & Coffee cup made Jenn's stomach tighten even more.

Taking a deep breath to try to bolster her courage, she said, "Liz, I'm sure you heard about what happened Saturday at Tamara's café."

"I did, and I'm so sorry you had to go through that. It must have been rough, having your ex insist on meeting with you like that."

Liz looked truly concerned. But not about Married in

Malibu's reputation—about Jenn. She knew she shouldn't have been so surprised by Liz's kindness, and the way she put her employees' happiness before the bottom line. But after having been so alone for so long, it was still sometimes hard to remember that she wasn't anymore.

"It was pretty rough," Jenn admitted. "But I want you to know nothing like that will ever happen again."

"I sure hope not. From what Tamara said, your ex was way over the line, trying to get you to stay and listen to his nonsense when you were ready to walk away."

"Unfortunately," Jenn said with a sigh, "that's just how Oliver is. But I dealt with it."

"I'm glad to hear it." Liz put her hand on Jenn's arm. "And I want you to know that if he ever tries to pull something like that again, give me a call and I'll come back you up. I'm sure everyone here feels the same."

Before she could think better of it, Jenn threw her arms around Liz. "Thank you for being a great boss. And for being a wonderful friend too."

"You're great, Jenn. Exactly the kind of strong woman I love to have on my team." Liz squeezed her tight as she added, "Don't let anyone ever tell you otherwise."

Jenn could feel herself starting to tear up at how deeply Liz's words touched her. It was exactly what she needed to hear this morning. But while it was one thing to hug her boss out of the blue, it was another to cry on her shoulder first thing in the morning.

"I'm sure you're busy, and I should get to work on the cakes."

Liz gave her a long look before nodding. "I'll be by to check in with you later. I meant it when I said I wanted to make sure you're not burning yourself out. Especially since I know the *Brides* spread is going to lead to plenty of big weddings in the future."

As Jenn hurried off toward the kitchen, she couldn't have been more thankful for all the work she had to do. Making wedding cakes for Married in Malibu's celebrity weddings was a huge honor, especially considering that she would have been baking every day anyway simply because she loved it so much. And considering how crazy her personal life had been recently, it was no small relief to know that she could retreat to her kitchen and focus on her cakes.

Today in particular, she needed to put every single ounce of focus into making sure the *Brides* shoot was as perfect as possible. But when she stepped into her kitchen, the first thing she saw wasn't her cakes.

It was Daniel.

He looked so good standing there, with the sun from the kitchen windows lighting him up from behind. But nothing could match the brightness of the smile he gave her, one that was filled with so much love it took her breath away.

When he opened his arms, there was no way she could have stopped herself from stepping into them. He was so strong. So steady. So wonderful.

Suddenly, she couldn't bottle up her emotions another moment. She started to cry, tears spilling down her cheeks as he held her. Normally, she hated crying. It always felt as though she'd lost control and people would see her as weak.

Yet, with Daniel, it didn't feel like that. In his arms, she felt safe.

Like she'd finally come home.

★ ★ ★

"It's going to be okay," Daniel whispered.

There was so much more he wanted to say, but for now he simply wanted her to know that if she ever needed him, he would be there. Giving her space to process everything yesterday had been one of the hardest things he'd ever done. He'd nearly called her, nearly gone to her apartment, a dozen times. But he'd known that wasn't fair. He couldn't force her to love him back—only Jenn could make that decision for herself.

A short while later, she drew away. Despite the tears still streaking her cheeks, she bravely said, "I think we need to talk."

After they both pulled out stools and were sitting facing each other, he wanted to reach for her hand. But he couldn't. Not until he knew if she returned his feelings.

Or if she didn't.

"Oliver was waiting for me at my apartment when I got home on Saturday."

Daniel couldn't disguise his shock. He was furious that her ex would dare ambush her like that, especially after she'd already let him know at Tamara's café that she wasn't interested.

Calling on his self-control to keep from ranting about what a waste of oxygen Oliver was, he asked, "What happened?"

"I finally got him to understand that not only do I not want to see him again, I don't want to be with him. *Ever* again." Certainty, and obvious relief, rang behind every word she spoke. "I didn't even realize until yesterday that my marriage was an anchor I thought I needed to keep dragging around with me. I'd built the final break into an impossible thing in my head. Yet when the time came to tell Oliver that we really were done forever, it didn't end up being hard at all." She was silent for a moment before adding, "I guess I kept thinking that if I couldn't make things work with Oliver, there must be something wrong with me. Something broken."

"You're anything but broken," Daniel said softly. "Your strength astounds me every day. But I understand how difficult it is to let go of the past. When I lost Victoria, it felt as though there was something fundamentally wrong with the world. In those early years, I kept going only because my kids needed me. For so long, even thinking about being happy again felt like a betrayal. And I didn't want to let anyone new into the family dynamic. Not only because I didn't want to trust someone else with my kids' hearts when they needed me more than ever after losing their mom, but also because I couldn't stand the thought of losing anyone else. How could I be sure that the next woman I loved wouldn't just be taken away from me again?"

"I haven't wanted to risk putting my heart on the line either," she admitted. "I mean, if I couldn't see what was wrong with my husband, how could I be sure about anyone else? How could I be sure it wouldn't happen again? But you know what I'm starting to realize?" She reached out her hand and slid it into his. "Even though the end of my marriage was painful, not everything that came out of it was bad. If Oliver and I hadn't split up, if I hadn't had to take a long hard look at my life, if I hadn't had to start over, I might not be here now doing what I love." She put her other hand in Daniel's before adding, "And if I hadn't come to Married in Malibu, I would never have met you."

Daniel wanted to lean over and kiss her with all of the emotion, all of the passion, he'd been holding back for far too long. But first, he needed her to know something. "I never thought that I would fall in love again. I never thought that I would meet anyone who would be worth taking that kind of risk for." He drew her closer, so close that his mouth was almost against hers, as he said, "Until you."

At the same time that she wound her arms around his neck, he slid his around her waist. And when she pressed her lips against his, it was the sweetest, most tender kiss Daniel had ever experienced.

How long they kissed, Daniel didn't know. All he knew was her taste, her scent, her softness, the happy little sound she made when he pulled her closer. He wished he didn't have to let her go.

But he did, because they were in the middle of Married in Malibu's commercial kitchen. Clearly, she had the realization at the same moment he did. They were both laughing when they finally sat back.

"Liz told me not to burn myself out today. Which means we're going to need to take plenty of kissing breaks." She gave him a sexy little smile as she ran her fingers through his hair.

He couldn't resist stealing another kiss. More like ten, actually. Even though they did need to get back to work. Because the *Brides* shoot wouldn't wait.

But he would. He'd meant it when he said he would wait as long as it took for her to be able to love him back the way he loved her. Considering that it had only been hours since she'd resolved things completely with her ex, it made perfect sense that she hadn't burst out with an *I love you* this morning.

Of course, he hoped to hear her say those three little words soon, but just knowing that she trusted him enough to risk any part of her heart at all already made him feel like the luckiest guy in the world.

* * *

By the end of the day, all three cakes were nearly completely constructed and iced. The theme-park cake looked like a fairy-tale castle. The traditional wedding cake stood proud and multi-tiered, stretching up so high that Jenn planned to disassemble it before she left for the night so that she wouldn't have to worry about it collapsing. Only the Malibu cake wasn't quite there yet.

Throughout the day, Daniel had worked his magic, taking dozens of helpful test shots for the magazine shoot, and plenty of candids of her too. She'd never been entirely comfortable in front of a camera, but he made it seem so natural that she often found herself forgetting he was capturing her every move.

It didn't hurt, of course, that she loved having him close like this. She couldn't help but want to kiss him, couldn't keep from reaching out to touch him. And when he wrapped his arms around her late in the afternoon while she worked a delicate spiral into one of the layers of icing, her heart felt so full she thought it might burst.

He pressed a kiss to the top of her head. "I need to head out to pick the kids up. They're over at a friend's house, and Adam texted to say I'd better get there before the girls give him a makeover."

"I never had a sibling, but I'm sure that's some sort of big sister, little brother rite of passage, isn't it?" Jenn said with a laugh as she turned to put her arms around his waist. "I'd love it if you would say hello to them for me and also let them know I'm really looking forward to seeing them again."

"I know they'd like the same thing. They both adore you."

"It's mutual." She'd fallen for Daniel's kids just as fast as she'd fallen for their father. "I wish I could come with you tonight, but I still have a few things to finish up for tomorrow. I want everything to be perfect."

"You've done amazing work, Jenn." He gave her a reassuring smile as he gently brushed back the hair that had come loose from her ponytail. "You don't need to be nervous about anything. The shoot is going to go great."

The kiss he gave her was so sweet she wished it could go on forever. But when his phone dinged again with another text from his son, she shooed him out the door.

Her stomach was still fluttering from his kiss when she headed back across the kitchen to study her Malibu cake. On the plus side, the ocean and shore both seemed lifelike. But she couldn't stop feeling that something was missing. If only she could figure out what.

"How's it going?"

She turned to find Liz standing in the doorway. "Really well...apart from the Malibu cake, that is."

Liz walked into the kitchen, exclaiming over the beauty of the theme-park cake and the traditional cake before stopping in front of the Malibu cake.

They were both silently studying it when Jenn said, "I've been racking my brain to figure out what's missing with this one. But I haven't been able to yet."

"Then it's probably time for you to take a break," Liz suggested. "Why don't we go get a coffee?"

Ordinarily, going over to Tamara's for a few minutes would have seemed like a lifesaver. But Jenn still felt more than a little embarrassed by what had happened there with Oliver and Daniel.

As if she could read her mind, Liz said, "Trust me, coffee is just what you need to clear your head—and to make you realize that no one is at all upset with you for what happened at the café on Saturday. Now come on. You're coming across the street with me. That's an order."

"Yes, boss," Jenn said as Liz steered her toward the door.

Fortunately, Liz was right and no one stared at Jenn as they picked out a table by the window, not even the regulars who had been in that weekend.

"I'll bring your coffees over," Tamara called out. She soon brought not only drinks for the three of them, but also a slice of lemon cake that looked absolutely delicious. She slid it in front of Jenn. "I thought you might be so busy making cakes that you've forgotten to eat any of them."

Jenn's stomach growled right on cue, and she happily forked a bite into her mouth. "Mmmm," she said around a mouth full of deliciousness. "This is incredible. I feel like I just walked into a sunny lemon orchard. Who made it?"

"It's my grandmother's secret recipe. Play your cards right," she said with a wink, "and I just might be convinced to share it with you."

"Just tell me what I need to do," Jenn said, ready to beg if it came to that. Tamara's grandmother's lemon cake was *that* good.

"All I want is for you to tell me how you're doing," Tamara said. "I was really worried about you, but I didn't want to hover when you needed time to process everything."

"I guess I'm still a little stunned by how messy things got." Messy enough that even though she and Daniel were now officially a couple, she still hadn't been brave enough to put her entire heart on the line yet.

"I know all about messes," Liz said. "Look at how complicated things got with me and Jason when we were falling back in love..."

Love.

The word resonated deep within Jenn's chest. Once upon a time, she'd been so sure that she knew what love was. With Oliver, even from the start of their marriage, love had been a weight, an anchor, keeping her tethered to a bad relationship. And when he'd betrayed her trust, she'd come to associate love with the stabbing ache of betrayal. She'd closed her heart to try to shut those feelings out, but the ache had still been there, along with all the painful memories.

But then she'd come to Married in Malibu, where she'd made friends, good ones. And where she'd met Daniel.

Just thinking of him made her smile, her smile growing even wider as she remembered the feel of his lips pressing against hers.

"Oh my," Tamara said with a smile of her own, "someone definitely has it bad."

"I do." The words left Jenn's lips before she could overthink them, or hold them back out of fear. At long last, she realized that even worries about bumps that might appear in future roads couldn't possibly beat out the strength of her feelings. "I'm in love with Daniel."

"At last!" Liz said at the exact moment that Tamara said, "Finally!"

Jenn laughed as the women high-fived. "That obvious, is it?"

"Yes, it is," Tamara said. "But it's easy for us to say when we've been watching from the sidelines. I can only imagine how happy he's going to be when you finally tell him how you feel." She snapped her fingers as if she'd had a great idea. "Maybe you could surprise him by baking a cake in the shape of a heart or something?"

Just like that, the perfect idea hit Jenn so hard and fast that she nearly fell off her chair. "Tamara, you're a genius!" She hugged her friend. "I need to get back to the kitchen right away." She was already halfway to the door when she turned to say, "Thank you for everything, guys. You're the best."

At long last, she knew not only how to fix her Malibu cake—but also how to let Daniel know that she loved him with her entire heart and every last piece of her soul.

Love had shown her the way.

Chapter Sixteen

"Thank you for taking a chance on me and my cakes." Jenn shook hands with Bryan, the *Brides* photographer, and Grace, the editor overseeing the wedding cake spread. A small army of people from the magazine had descended on Married in Malibu for the day. "I hope you like what I've created for the shoot."

"Everyone we've spoken to says your work is spectacular." Grace gestured to Daniel. "Particularly your biggest fan over here."

Jenn's cheeks flushed as she smiled at Daniel. "I couldn't have gotten ready for today without his help."

"We're ready to begin shooting whenever you are." Bryan was a young, hungry photographer who reminded Daniel of himself in the early years. Ready and willing to shoot anything.

Seeing the nerves on Jenn's beautiful face, Daniel sent her a silent message: *I'm so proud of you. Now go knock their socks off.* He knew she'd understood him when she nodded, then turned to the photographer and said, "I'm ready."

The first cake Jenn unveiled was the theme-park cake. "Wow," the editor said. "I've seen a lot of people try to take this on, but with your cake I almost feel like I'm a little girl again, dreaming of princes and princesses."

Jenn beamed. "I was hoping for exactly that reaction."

Next, she moved to the traditional cake. Nate had helped build a large cover for it, and she needed Daniel's help to lift it free. Both the editor and the photographer gasped at the beautifully decorated five-level wedding cake.

"You really are an artist, Jenn." Bryan was clearly impressed. "I don't know if I could bring myself to cut into this and eat it. I'd want to find a way to preserve it forever."

"Thank you. That's so nice of you."

She was clearly pleased with everyone's compliments. But when she moved to stand beside the third cake, instead of looking more relaxed, it almost seemed as if her nerves multiplied many times over.

"For my final cake, I wanted to do something really special. Married in Malibu has a private beach cove where our brides and grooms can say their vows, and that spot has become one of my favorite places in the world." She was looking straight at Daniel as she said,

"It's where I finally learned what love is really all about. Love can sometimes be scary and messy, but it's also the most beautiful thing in the world. And worth absolutely any risk."

As she lifted the cover from the cake, everyone in the room moved closer to take in the stunning details. Her representation of the ocean and the sandy shoreline out of icing and cake was nothing short of brilliant. But for Daniel, it was the new additions that truly made the cake stand out.

At the heart of the cake stood a man and a woman. The man had a camera around his neck, and the woman wore an apron smudged with chocolate. Two children— a boy and a girl who looked like Adam and Kayla— played in the sand while the man and woman held hands and gazed into each other's eyes.

He'd hoped she would say *I love you* soon. He should have known that when she did, it would be in a totally original—and incredibly sweet—way.

"I didn't think you could outdo the other two cakes," Bryan said before Daniel could tell Jenn how much her grand gesture—and her love—meant to him. "But you've just proved me wrong. The light is absolutely perfect right now, and I'd like to shoot as much as we can before anything changes. Let's start with this cake."

Daniel wanted to pull her into his arms and kiss her breathless. But she'd put everything she had into getting these cakes ready for today's shoot. She deserved to relish every second of her incredibly well-deserved big day. As soon as the shoot was done, she was all his.

And he was looking forward to loving her—and being loved by her—for the rest of their lives.

For now, the best he could do was slide his hand into hers for a brief moment before the bustling *Brides* staff drew them apart to consult on different issues.

Daniel was used to shoots where the magazine staff adjusted the sets a half-dozen times before eventually putting them back the way they originally were. Meg had knocked the backdrops out of the park, but even so she was happy to let the crew make changes if needed. Presently, two food and layout stylists were holding color charts and saying, "What do you think? More of the blue? Or do you think we should highlight the hints of gold in the sand?"

One by one, each of the Married in Malibu staff came to check out the shoot. Given that there was so little time in which to make things work, *Brides* had thrown everything at this spread. And just like he'd expected, Jenn had blown their expectations out of the water.

Several hours later, Jenn asked Daniel, "Is all this normal?" She'd been dashing around making constant adjustments to her cakes as the editor or photographer suggested new things. "Do you think things are going okay?"

"They're going *great*." He had to kiss her then, one small kiss that meant absolutely everything. Not only because he still could hardly believe that she was really his, but also because Liz and everyone else at Married in Malibu was clearly so happy to see them finally get together. "This much effort being put into the shoot means that your cakes are going to be a big deal in the magazine." He kissed her again. "You deserve every second of it."

As she stared up at him with her heart in her eyes, it felt as if they were the only people in the room. She opened her mouth to speak, but before she could say a word, Grace called her over to the theme-park cake to detail the ingredients she'd used to make the sparkles on the castle's roof.

"Is it just me," Kate said a while later when she came in from the garden, "or is it hot in here?"

Daniel had been so preoccupied with making sure that Jenn was okay while the photographer took hundreds of shots of the theme park and Malibu cakes from every possible angle, that he hadn't noticed the rising temperature in the room. But now that Kate mentioned it, he realized it really was hot with the setting sun streaming in through the windows. "I wonder if the AC is down?"

"I'll ask Nate to take a look at it," Kate said. During the past month, Nate had proved to be nearly as good a handyman as he was a computer expert.

Kate had only just left when Jenn rushed across the room. "Does it look to you like the traditional cake is leaning?"

Sure enough, it was slowly becoming a leaning tower of cake. The heat must have softened it, weakening its structural integrity.

"We need to hurry," Jenn said, panic beginning to overtake her earlier glow, "but Bryan just set up his equipment by the Malibu cake again." It had, unsurprisingly, proved to be everyone's favorite of the three cakes. Not only because it was stunning, but also because it was full of so much heart. "Is there any way that you can step in and make sure we get a few shots of this cake before it falls over? I know Bryan has taken some, but he's spent far less time with this one today."

Daniel didn't waste another second before picking up one of the cameras and dropping to one knee to take shots the way he would have in a war zone. Working with utter concentration, he took one picture after another. After working so closely with Jenn this week, he had some pretty good ideas about how to best showcase her work, so he was able to work very efficiently. Unfortunately, as the seconds ticked by, the cake was leaning more and more, the icing and cake growing softer with every degree the thermometer edged higher.

When the collapse came, it almost seemed to happen

in slow motion. The middle layer went first. As it slipped, the top layers came down, crashing into the bottom one. One of the photography assistants made an admirable attempt to catch it, but only ended up covered in cake for her trouble.

Daniel expected Jenn to be distraught. He reached out, intending to comfort her. But when he put his arms around her, she wasn't crying as she buried her head against his chest. She was laughing.

"So much for preserving the cake forever," she said through her laughter.

"Please tell me we have enough photos of this cake," the editor said.

Without letting go of Jenn, Daniel handed over the digital camera he'd taken the last-second pictures with.

Jenn drew back enough to be able to look up into his eyes. "I love you, Daniel. And I love Adam and Kayla too. There's nothing I want more than to be a part of your lives."

"We want that too. And they're going to be beside themselves with happiness at being immortalized on your cake. Just like I am."

"I've always loved baking, but never more than when I was working to capture your beautiful family."

Her mouth was soft and sweet beneath his as the chaos in the room momentarily faded away. Not long after, the shoot finally wound down, and Liz broke out a bottle of champagne to celebrate.

"To Jenn," Liz said as she lifted her glass. "The best cake designer anyone could hope for."

"To Jenn!" Daniel's voice was nearly drowned out by the others.

It didn't matter that the cake had collapsed. Life, as they both knew so well, was often messy. Sometimes you were able to laugh about it, other times you needed a good cry. But what mattered most was that they had their family. Their friends.

And *love*.

"Jenn," the editor said after she'd polished off her glass of champagne, "we're very glad we get to be the publication that 'discovered' your wedding cakes. And Daniel, you took some very impressive photos of the traditional cake in the heat of the moment."

"I'm just glad I could help."

Turning to Liz, Grace noted, "You've got yourself a very impressive staff."

"I certainly do," Liz agreed as she topped up Grace's glass.

"Jenn," Bryan said as he also accepted a bubbly refill, "Grace and I were talking, and we'd like to include a bio and photo of you with the shots of the cakes. Would it be possible to set up another shoot with just you?"

This was another thing Daniel had expected to happen. "I've been taking pictures of Jenn in the kitchen working on her cakes throughout the entire week if you'd like to see them."

Sixty seconds later, they had his camera plugged into the editor's laptop. As they looked at the shots Daniel had taken to document Jenn's creation process, he was utterly captivated by how happy she looked as she'd done everything from mixing batter to testing icing colors.

But as he looked more closely at the pictures, he suddenly realized her joy wasn't the only thing he'd captured with his camera during the week they'd spent working together in her kitchen. In the shots where she was looking straight at him, there was love there too.

So much love it took his breath away.

Jenn drew him away from the computer where Grace and Bryan were debating which pictures to use. "Do you think anyone would notice if we snuck out to the beach?"

They hurried out of the room before anyone could protest. Hand in hand, they headed down to the cove. The waves were gently crashing against the shore, and the setting sun had turned the sky an awe-inspiring purple.

"The last time we were here," she said softly, "you told me that you loved me. I thought I needed to be extra careful, that I needed to take things as slowly as possible, that I needed to examine starting a new relationship from every possible angle. But those pictures you took show what my heart always knew—that I've loved you from the first moment we met."

"Just the way I've always loved you." The kiss they shared was both sweet and sinful, simply perfect in every way. "We both have complicated pasts, but the only thing that matters is that the future has you in it."

"What do think your kids will say when they find out their matchmaking was a success?"

He grinned at the woman who was the second chance at love he'd never expected to get. "They're going to feel like all of their dreams have come true. Just like I do."

Epilogue

The moment *Brides* magazine hit the newsstands, everything went into overdrive at Married in Malibu. It wasn't just Jenn's incredible cakes that captured the public's imagination, it was the romantic pictures that the magazine had included of her with Daniel.

"First Liz and Jason, now Jenn and Daniel," Travis said to himself as he did his nightly walk around the perimeter of the Married in Malibu property to ensure that security was as tight as it could possibly be.

Of course, he'd expected plenty of romance at a wedding venue. He just hadn't thought each of the staff would fall in love one by one. Who would be next?

Would it be Kate, finally taking more of an interest in a man than her plants and flowers? Maybe Meg would suddenly emerge like a butterfly from her cocoon because of someone special? Or perhaps Nate would finally admit why he spent so much time at Tamara's coffee shop?

Whoever came next, Travis was sure it wouldn't be

him.

In any case, more publicity meant more business, which was great, but it also meant a marked increase in photographers trying to worm their way into getting shots of celebrities. Thankfully, the previous Saturday, Greta Sanserre's wedding had gone off without a hitch. No paparazzi had been able to enter the premises, and there hadn't been any sight lines through the bushes or the trees for the sneakier members of the press to get a shot of the happy couple or their guests.

Travis wasn't one to rest on his laurels, however. He believed in constantly upgrading security. With the rough neighborhood he'd grown up in, he'd learned that the smallest mistake, even letting down your guard for the briefest moment, meant that people could get hurt.

Married in Malibu's main building was fairly easy to keep locked down and under wraps, but an outdoor environment had many more variables. He wanted to have a new set of hidden security cameras installed by the time they put on their next wedding, this one for a supermodel.

He'd only just begun to prep the site when clouds started to roll in. California didn't get that many storms, but when the sky looked like this, you headed inside or you got soaked to the skin. Grabbing the expensive equipment, he sprinted toward the building, but made it inside a beat too late, the wall of rain drenching him in less than five seconds.

He was shaking the rain off when he heard knocking at the front door. In weather like this, one of the other Married in Malibu employees would probably have been tempted to throw the doors open and invite whoever was out there inside as quickly as possible. But Travis' security procedures were there for a reason. He made his way over to the camera feeds to see who was outside.

Rain pelted the woman standing at the door. The light wasn't great, but even so, there was no mistaking who she was.

Amy Woodford.

He hadn't seen her in years...but he'd never been able to forget the woman who had completely stolen his heart.

★ ★ ★ ★ ★

For news on upcoming books, sign up for Lucy Kevin's New Release Newsletter: LucyKevin.com/Newsletter

ABOUT THE AUTHOR

When *New York Times* and *USA Today* bestseller Lucy Kevin released her first novel, SEATTLE GIRL, it became an instant bestseller. All of her subsequent sweet contemporary romances have been hits with readers as well, including WHEN IT'S LOVE (*A Walker Island Romance*) which debuted at #1. Having been called "One of the top writers in America" by The Washington Post, she recently launched the very romantic *Married in Malibu* series. Lucy also writes contemporary romances as Bella Andre, and her incredibly popular series about The Sullivans has produced #1 bestsellers around the world, with more than 5 million books sold so far! If not behind her computer, you can find her swimming, hiking, or laughing with her husband and two children. For a complete listing of books, as well as excerpts and contests and to connect with Lucy:

Sign up for Lucy's Newsletter
LucyKevin.com